SETAN SERIES:
BOOK 2

THE HAVEN

SANDY WEST

Copyright © 2025 Loch Saticama Publishing
All Rights Reserved
Cover: Miblart
Editor: Rachael Swanson
ISBN-13: 979-8-9996528-3-6 (eBook)
ISBN-13: 979-8-9996528-4-3 (print)
ISBN-13: 979-8-9996528-5-0 (hardcover)

Acknowledgements

Thank you to all those who believed in me and to all my lovely readers. I can't do it without your support. All my love to my supportive children and family. Another thanks goes out to my editor, Rachael. Once this series is done, I'll get working on *that* book.

The Haven

1

AS JACOB STOWED THE last of their gear, the chill of the morning air bit at his cheeks. He could see his breath puffing out in white clouds. Although spring had sprung, the mornings still held the crisp, cold smell of winter, a stark contrast to the budding flowers. He knew they would for a while. The curse—or perk—of living in Maine. His favorite part of the day was the peace of the early morning. The silence meant no one was awake, and he heard no cars. The house was up on a hill—not so great in winter—within a rural subdivision. Both he and his sister preferred to be out of the city, and had grown up here.

Birdsong signaled their return from the south. He knew it would increase as the temperature warmed. The wind swayed the tall pines, swirling his short curls in its dance. The number of trees meant you couldn't see much of your neighbors, which his family had always liked. His eyes glanced at the houses he could see, remembering several going up, the construction breaking the solitude.

When his parents had purchased the property, the street had been bare. Their house was the first to be built. Now, every lot had one.

Thankfully, the lots were larger, so that kept the houses spread apart. As he looked up, he noticed the pine next to the house had holes running up its trunk.

I'll have that looked at when we get back. Could be carpenter ants. If it fell on the house...

He glanced at his state-of-the-art watch, noticing the time. Her shift was almost over. In the past, she was often late due to charting. Today, the AI completing charting allowed her to leave work promptly, avoiding the usual overtime crunch. He returned to the garage, verifying that he had packed everything on the holographic list hovering near him, unconsciously stroking his trimmed auburn beard as he read.

Once again, he wished Sia would agree to a house-bot, then he wouldn't be out here freezing his butt off packing. He'd tried talking her into it several times, but his sister was adamant about not having an AI housekeeper. While he loved being outside in all kinds of weather, he was feeling overwhelmed. It could load the car while he edited and uploaded his social media videos. He needed to schedule their release on time while they were gone.

As he stepped inside the pale-yellow Colonial, his phone and watch chimed a notification. Dollars to doughnuts, it was her.

Almost done. ETA an hour-ish.

He breathed a sigh of relief, happy she hadn't backed out of their plans. It took him forever to get her to agree to some time away from her job. Her compassion caused her to feel guilty about taking any vacation time, given their current staffing issues. Those issues may soon be resolved. With the nursing shortage reaching crisis levels, the clamor to produce and release dependable nurse-bots was fierce among competing companies. Technically, they were called Advanced Medical Protocol AI, but no one wanted to say that mouthful. Since they were in the testing phase, very few knew what AMPA meant outside of those creating them and those who followed AI progress, like himself. Jacob knew that she, as well as others, were also worried about being replaced. Daily, outside the companies, protesters—mostly medical personnel in scrubs—marched, their chants echoing through the streets.

Entering the house, his eyes were drawn upward to the holographic tablet near the garage door, where a message flickered to life with a soft glow, the quiet whir of its mechanics barely audible. Mom. Having given her children the family home following their father's death, she moved to the warmer South, hoping the milder climate would ease her arthritic joints. Both siblings missed her. She had a wicked sense of humor and knew how to make them laugh after a bad day. Plus, she was an excellent cook.

The summit they were hiking this trip was high, so they'd be out of reach for about a week. His sister refused to use the latest phone tech to increase their signal, which was fine. They agreed to shut them off to concentrate on family and nature, though they would bring their solar chargers so they could take pictures without their phones dying. They wanted a full reset of their bodies and minds.

Better talk to Mom now.

His finger tapped the air in front of him and began the short video call with their mother. The screen switched to 3-D mode, making their mother look like a disembodied head with a sitting room background.

"Hey, Mom! How's the weather?"

"I'm about to bake cookies in the mailbox. How are things with you? Still cold?"

He chuckled at her way of saying it was hot. "Just in the mornings. The days are warming."

Her short gray hair bobbed as she nodded, and he could see her aide-bot moving in the background. "How's the bot working out?"

"Great. It's like my mother has been reborn." She had a sarcastic edge to her voice. "Couldn't you guys have gotten me one of the other bots? I'm not getting any younger, you know. I could use a little fun."

"Mom!" He did not need that mental image in his head.

"What? I'm old, not dead." She winked at him.

Jacob's hand rubbed his face. He hadn't drunk enough coffee for this.

They switched their discussion to the trip timeline, so she knew when to expect them back. If they weren't back within twenty-four hours of that, she would call the park rangers. Jacob had learned during his many expeditions into the wild that you always tell at least one person where you are and when you'll be back.

"I have an emergency GPS locator on my watch." He raised it to show her. "If anything happens, I'll activate it."

She nodded, then her face grew serious. "I'm glad you talked Sia into taking time off. I was getting concerned about her. She's overworking herself."

Jacob agreed.

They talked for a short time, then said their goodbyes.

After they disconnected, Jacob contemplated sending that bot to his mom as a joke. Though knowing her, she would most likely use it, then brag about it. That was not something he wanted to hear.

2

SIANA RUBBED THE BACK of her neck to ease the tension, avoiding the tracker as she walked to the nurses' station. Though it was under her skin—a small rectangular chip—she could feel it. She hated the thing and never wanted it. Unfortunately, their government had insisted you have one or you couldn't get a job, shop, or do much of anything. It had started with the children. Targeting individuals with disabilities, they emphasized their increased vulnerability by exploiting the fears of abduction, being lost, and even death. Who wouldn't want a nonverbal autistic child tracked?

After that, they made it a requirement for school entry and pediatric appointments. Soon they targeted the adults. First, it was the elderly who tended to wander off, unable to remember their own names. It trickled through to the rest of the population. They wanted to "make it easier for the country." How, she didn't know. The thought of AI programs meticulously tracking her every move, purchase, work schedule, and even her salary was deeply disturbing. Facing unemployment, debt, and hunger, she joined the queue. She often regretted that decision. Especially now that the nurse-bots were becoming a likely possibility. She may lose her job anyway.

The Haven

She found herself looking forward to her camping vacation, though she had first refused. Jacob hadn't backed down. As twins, they were equally stubborn. He encouraged her to go off for some sibling bonding with him. Even as they grew older, they made sure to carve out time, playing board games until late at night or sharing popcorn and whispers during a quiet movie. As they both went to college, it became harder to do so. After they started their respective jobs, the time they spent together dwindled, despite sharing a home to save money. The quiet evenings and shared meals were now a distant memory, replaced by the hurried rush of separate schedules.

His reminder that it had been years since her last vacation, spoken with a warmth that eased her guilt, persuaded her to agree to the trip. She was feeling burned out and needed one, though guilt still ate at her. They were short-staffed as it was. Now they'd be down another. She reminded herself it was only for a week. Nothing would happen that the others wouldn't be able to handle. They all had the same training.

As she reached the station, a cleaner-bot rolled around the end, causing both of them to stop in their tracks. The absence of their regular human cleaning crew left a noticeable void. The hospital judged AI cleaners to be more cost-effective than hiring humans. Siana had her doubts. One breaking down made it difficult to keep things clean. The hospital lacked funds for a backup. Despite its status as the state's largest hospital, it paled compared to urban counterparts nationwide. Its income didn't support the cost.

This bot was the height of an average human with a matte finish. Because studies revealed the shiny surfaces caused anxiety in many humans, manufacturers toned down the colors, resulting in a less reflective, more muted appearance. Their faces, which were the most basic, made her uneasy. Lifeless eyes sat above multiple holes near the bottom of their "face." Their version of a mouth. It felt like part of a horror movie to her, yet others were unconcerned. Their colors denoted their jobs, and their eye color matched. Fancier models boasted faces resembling computer monitors, their sleek screens displaying various expressions. What bothered her was the fact that they were making some that looked human. They wanted them identical to where no one would be able to tell them apart.

How long before we're all replaced?

Her jaw tightened at the thought.

At least we don't have drones watching us like the schools do, though that could change.

Mel, one of the other nurses, turned toward her, a familiar face playing on her phone. It was one of her sibling's social media videos.

"Sia, seriously. You need to introduce me to your brother already."

"I told you, he's not looking for anyone."

Mel insisted on this at least once a week. Siana couldn't handle it right now. Exhaustion overwhelmed her. She was also fairly certain it was the fact her brother had over two million followers that prompted it. Mel embraced popular culture. Her brother was an easy target. That he was attractive also helped.

"I'm telling you. Let me meet him. I'll change his mind." Mel gave what was supposed to be a seductive look, but it made her look constipated.

With a roll of her eyes, Siana gathered her gear. "You can always buy yourself a sex-bot," she shot back.

"Like I could afford that!" Mel scoffed. "Plus, I like warmth."

"You can get warming models."

"No, thanks. I like real men. Not plastic or metal." Mel gave an exaggerated shiver. "Though with them making bots more human-like, I might save up for one." Mel seemed to lose herself in thought.

Probably planning how she'd design it. Siana chuckled to herself, yet a twinge of unease settled in her.

Human interaction kept dropping as people turned to the bots for more and more of their needs. The hospital had to open a special wing for those having mental breakdowns over not having their AI "friends" along with other issues that came from AI.

Mel was a good friend, and Siana wished her well while she was gone. As Sia departed, she offered her coworker and the rest of the morning crew a quiet smile and a wish for an uneventful day.

Mel's own eyes rolled as she said, "Hush! You know better than to say that."

It was a useless wish; pediatrics was never uneventful. The elevator dinged, a late nurse exited, and Siana ran to catch it. A doctor saw her coming and held the door. She dove in and thanked him.

"Just getting off?" he asked with a hopeful expression.

"Yeah."

She didn't want to talk. With her eyes closed, she rested against the elevator wall. He remained quiet, thankfully. Although she knew him and he seemed nice, she wasn't interested in a relationship, just like her brother. This doctor—she was struggling to recall his name—had been flirting with her of late, his interest obvious. Her number one rule was never to get involved with a doctor at work. She'd seen it backfire spectacularly on more than one occasion.

The familiar ding of the elevator signaled her stop. As the doors opened, the harsh fluorescent lights of the parking garage illuminated rows of cars, the sounds of distant engines hummed in the background, and exhaust fumes wafted over her. She waved goodbye and hurried to her car, her footsteps echoing. Exhausted and yearning for sleep, she still had the tasks of getting home, finishing packing, and loading everything into Jacob's car. She was glad to have finished most of the packing before work last night, so it wouldn't take long. She would sleep in the car as he drove.

With the city still waking, the morning air was crisp and the traffic leaving the urban center was minimal, a peaceful end to her day. Noticing her gas tank was low, she stopped at the gas station. As the gas-bot came to her window, she rolled it down.

"How much?" This one was a bit more informal than the others.

She said, "Fill up, please."

It reached a "hand" forward and scanned her tracker. They were linked to their bank accounts.

"Siana Landon confirmed. Payment pending. You worked a thirteen-hour shift. One hour longer than scheduled. Are you tired?"

"No, I'm fine. Thank you," she said, forcing a smile.

"Would you like a car wash today? It has been forty-seven days since your last one."

"No, thanks."

Other than its questions, this was one AI bot she didn't mind. She hated pumping gas. Her side mirror showed her the bot's progress as she tried to suppress a yawn. She didn't want it to question whether or not she was too tired to drive. The last thing she needed was her car being taken, and Jacob having to fetch her. It had already happened twice. Sia hated the AI's micromanagement of their lives. How others were happy with it left her shaking her head, perplexed. She preferred her autonomy.

Before authorizing operation, any bot assisting with vehicles and people meticulously verified that the driver exhibited no signs of fatigue or intoxication. On the plus side, the integration of AI into most vehicles resulted in a significant decrease in drunk driving accidents. Upon registering alcohol, the car initiated a breathalyzer scan to determine the driver's blood alcohol content. If it deemed you were too drunk, the engine lock engaged. Even if you seemed fine but drove erratically, the system intervened, pulling the car over and disabling the engine. If it scanned a medical emergency, it called EMS. The overall sense of security was strong for those on the road, a stark difference from previous years.

How long before EMS is replaced?

Her car was older, so it didn't have the latest AI upgrades. She didn't want them anyway. She was convinced AI was already too intrusive. The thunk of her gas tank door being closed brought her attention back to the bot.

"Receipt sent. Have a good day."

It moved back into its alcove to wait for the next customer. Siana restarted her drive, her mind still thinking. While AI offered undeniable benefits, the sheer willingness of people to surrender their autonomy felt like a slow, steady descent into dependence; a coldness settling over society. AI wrote the books, music and made art. It seemed like there were subtle messages in all of them lately. Messages that leaned toward mankind becoming obsolete. People could no longer tell what video or audio was real and what was AI-created. The unemployment rate soared as AI took jobs, leaving many people struggling to make ends meet. Crime had escalated to unprecedented proportions. She kept bear spray in her purse and car at all times.

What she disliked most though were the data centers. The construction of enormous centers to run the programs and build and repair the bots resulted in the demolition of tons of farmland and forests. Initially, job creation via these centers excited local citizens. The employees were blissfully unaware that the first batch of bots they proudly assembled, with their smooth metal exteriors and quiet hums, took their jobs. Siana shoved the thoughts out of her mind. The subject frustrated her to the point where she felt a knot of tension forming in her stomach.

I'm supposed to be relaxing.

Forty-five minutes later, she pulled into the driveway of her childhood home. A glance at the clock on her dash showed her she was on time. The overhead garage door was still open, Jacob's car waiting to leave. She drove her car all the way inside. The door to the house slammed as she entered her home, tossing her belongings onto the nearby bench.

"You look like something the cat dragged in." Her brother examined her with a small amount of concern.

She tilted her head, auburn curls falling in front of her eyes, mock-glared at him, and said, "I'll be ready soon. I just need to finish packing."

With thudding footsteps, she ran upstairs. Her bedroom door swung open easily at her push. She hurried in and closed it, undressing as she moved toward the closet. Her scrubs fell to the floor as she grabbed a shirt and threw it on, adding a long-sleeved layer on top. Her hand yanked open her dresser drawer, the sound echoing in the quiet room, grabbed her favorite pair of denim jeans, and slipped them on. She donned her little-used hiking boots. After scooping her scrubs from the floor, she tossed them into the bathroom hamper. She loved having a house with two masters. It was something their parents insisted on when they built it, planning on hosting their own elderly parents when it was time. Now that Jacob and she owned the house, each had their own en suite bathroom. It cut down on arguments.

After placing her toothbrush and paste into a toiletry bag, she threw the bag into her duffel. As she picked up her backpack and duffel, she heard Jacob letting the dogs back inside from their bathroom break, their barking and jumping echoing through the house. They loved car rides and could always tell when they were going on one. Her eyes swept the room once more, double-checking she had left nothing behind. Her footsteps were quieter going down.

She hurried into the garage and threw her belongings into the back of Jacob's SUV, noting that he had already loaded everything else. The backseat was crammed with a cooler and two excited dogs, their fur shedding onto the leather. She leaned into the front passenger side to set down her purse and felt the happy slobber of a wet nose and warm tongue on her face.

"Panda!" Her voice held amusement.

The Haven

A joyous bark escaped the gray hound mix, his black-circled eyes shining with delight. She pulled her head back and sat down, the AI automatically buckling her seat belt, then she reclined the seat. She honestly hated Jacob's vehicle. Although the newest model was fully AI-controlled, it was the trip's best option. Her little sedan, while all-wheel drive, wouldn't have the space for everything.

Overwhelmed by fatigue, she shut her eyes. A dog snuffled her hair, but soon stopped as the driver's door opened. The smell of coffee preceded Jacob as he sat in the driver's seat. As exhaustion claimed her, she heard the car start. The quiet hum of the engine filled the garage as the AI shifted into gear, pulled out, and automatically closed the garage door, its mechanism whirring quietly, while Jacob pulled out his laptop, the keys clicking softly as he began editing videos, preferring to do it himself over using AI.

3

THEY JOINED A GROUP of hikers, their boots crunching on the worn dirt path as they began their ascent to the summit. Much to the dogs' displeasure, because of the sheer drop-offs, they were leashed. Jacob had wanted to buy AI leash collars for them, so the twins didn't need to carry actual leashes; they just had to put the owner's device in their pockets. It connected to a dog's special collar, keeping them invisibly leashed. Siana had been adamantly against it, so he'd dropped the subject. He never understood her resistance to what he considered progress. Not to mention the ease AI brought into their lives.

On the summit, buffeted by wind, they used their phones to capture images of the sunny vistas and themselves. The group felt dwarfed by the mountain's extensive range. Although the morning was cool, the wind felt good. The strenuous climb left everyone sweating, their clothes clinging to them despite the cool air. The group enjoyed themselves immensely. Jacob asked someone to take a picture of him and his sister to commemorate her first climb of that trail, cracking a joke just before the picture snapped, causing everyone to laugh. Since it was at Siana's expense, he received a slight punch to the arm from his sister.

The topic of trackers arose on the return trip down to their respective campsites. Jacob could see the surprise on Siana's face over the number of people who didn't mind them. He was one of them, but he knew she was uncomfortable with it. Siana's expression prompted a group member to speak up.

"They're going to use the trackers to kill humans."

A nervous chuckle escaped a couple of hikers.

"You don't believe me, but it's true. By finding you through the tracker, they can end your life. They're going to exterminate humans, take over the planet, then—if killing humans doesn't work—destroy it to start over. They feel we haven't learned our lesson."

An uncomfortable silence fell over the group, and the others hurried back to their campsites to get away from him, the jovial atmosphere gone. Jacob noticed Siana slowing to talk to the man. Jacob followed behind them as they went down the trail. He also noticed the dogs were staring at the man as they walked. That unnerved him. Jacob examined the stranger. He had nothing distinctive about him: brown hair, average build, just an average-looking guy wearing sunglasses against the glare of the day. He wore hiking boots, cargo pants, and layered tops similar to everyone else.

When the man passed her two metal things, he grew suspicious and called to her. "Sia, let's return to feed the dogs. It's past time."

A warm smile touched her lips as she thanked the man, then rejoined Jacob, their steps quickening as they hurried back to their campsite.

"He says these chokers can block the trackers." Her hand held them up for him to see, sunlight reflecting off the metal.

A silent chuckle rumbled in Jacob's chest as he nodded, careful not to hurt her feelings. She believed in the best of people. He wouldn't change that for the world. Despite her gentle nature, his twin's kindness was often exploited, leaving her feeling hurt and disappointed. He suspected the man was such a person.

"How much did you give him?" he asked. He knew she carried cash on her, though it was rarely used nowadays.

"Nothing," she said.

Her furrowed brow and hurried pace told him she didn't like his tone. He made her favorite campfire burgers for dinner as an apology. As they ate, they talked about the first camping trip they'd gone on with their father. Years after his passing from cancer, his absence was still deeply felt. He possessed a booming laugh: a powerful, resonant sound capable of startling anyone who didn't know him well.

"Your laugh sounds like his." Siana smiled in remembrance.

"Does it? I'm glad I got something from him." He chuckled.

"Mom always called us her 'mini-mes.'" Siana took another bite of her burger. "Oh, my gosh. How do you make such good campfire burgers? Mine always come out plain." She spoke with a mouthful, hand covering her lower face.

Jacob's face became overly serious as he leaned toward her and whispered, "It's a secret botanist recipe."

Giving him a look, she stated, "Dad was not a botanist."

They both knew he'd tweaked their father's recipe, adding a few of his own special touches.

As Jacob blatantly cheated during their later card game, Siana's exasperated yet good-natured yells filled the air. The sound of their laughter echoed through the campground as her clever retorts and his equally sharp comebacks bounced back and forth until both grew too sleepy to continue.

***

"Jacob!"

The sharp, insistent barking of dogs and his sister's urgent cries tore him from his slumber. She had come into his tent and was shaking him, her grip tight on his arm.

"What?" Sleep invaded his murmur.

"They're dying!"

He shot awake. "Who? What are you talking about?"

As he sat up, he felt the icy bite of the early morning air against his skin, the weak sun a pale ghost behind the tent's thin olive-green fabric.

"Put this on!" With a sharp movement, she thrust a choker toward him, narrowly missing his face.

He brushed it aside with the back of his hand, the other rubbing sleep away. "You're not making sense. What are you talking about?"

Silent tears tracked down her cheeks. Worried eyes stared back at him.

What is going on?

"Please! Just put it on! Make sure it covers the tracker. That's what he said they're for."

Her fear was palpable. Jacob could practically feel it radiating off of her. Even though he didn't know why, he put on the cold, metallic choker, adjusted it to fit, and concealed the tracker beneath it. He slid himself out of his sleeping bag, stood, and stretched his six-foot, two-inch frame as far as he could within the confines of the cabin tent, shivering slightly in the chill.

"I went to the bathroom. A fellow hiker was present. We started talking about other trails to climb. On our way back, we encountered a hiker we had been with the day before, lying on the ground with most of her head missing." She took a deep breath. "She wasn't the only one." Her voice trembled. "I walked ahead of the hiker and heard a loud noise. When I turned, something had blown her head apart."

"What?"

Jacob's jaw dropped, a stunned silence replacing the words that failed him. Siana didn't engage in flights of fancy. The distant screams and cries of other campers reached him, panicked and desperate. He realized he could hear them faintly, but clearly, and his concern escalated.

"Let me get dressed. I'll be out in a minute."

As she left, his mind raced, a whirlwind of confusion and unanswered questions.

Maybe bears?

He yanked off his sweats and threw on jeans, layered short and long-sleeved shirts, changed his socks, shoved his feet into his boots, and left the tent. A frenzy of barking and growling erupted from the dogs, though they remained near the tent. Their agitated energy vibrated in the air.

The twins had located a secluded campsite, preventing disruption; consequently, they remained visually unaware of unfolding events. The distant screams filtered and echoed through the trees. Small explosion-like noises were audible. With a shared look of dawning horror, brother and sister stood frozen, the unspoken question of what was going on hanging heavy in the air as they stared at one another, their hearts pounding. With a start, they watched a blur of motion. Wearing jeans and a long-sleeved shirt, the man who'd given Siana the chokers burst into the campsite, his frantic gestures punctuated by the sounds of his ragged breathing.

"They started earlier than expected. Come with me. Hurry!" His arm beckoned them before he spun and ran out of their site.

Jacob, hesitating, didn't trust the man. Siana, of course, ran after him.

"Sia!"

Because he had no choice, Jacob ran after her, with dogs in pursuit. She was so trusting; it felt like she didn't have a single protective instinct. As he ran, the sight of scattered bodies contrasted with the serene beauty of the New Hampshire forest, making him stop short. They were missing all or part of their heads, with blood and brain matter splattered around. A few had their heads lying near their bodies, necks torn apart.

Their shepherd mix, Cooper, whimpered. He was elderly and had health issues. This might be his last camping trip. It was one reason Jacob brought the dogs instead of boarding them. Cooper loved running in the woods, though he could no longer race with abandon. The siblings wanted to give him a few joys before his life was over. Jacob's eyes glanced at him, just confirming he was okay. His brown eyes stared back. The deaths distressed the canine.

What is going on right now?

His shocked gaze took in the sight before continuing to follow his sister. As he ran into the other man's campsite, the smell of wood smoke hung in the air, and he saw his sister disappearing into a beat-up, beige motorhome. He was continually surprised that no one had ever kidnapped her. He entered the motorhome after her, his eyes catching sight of the unusual layout while the dogs hesitated outside.

The current owner revamped it. He had crammed the entire living area, overflowing with furniture and belongings, into the front. In place of the standard RV sofa was a daybed made with a homemade quilt and pillow, and various items were stored in plastic cabinets and drawers, rattling slightly with every movement of the motorhome. His sister's back was moving to the rear bedroom; he followed. Jacob squeezed in beside her, his jaw dropping. The bedroom, a high-tech marvel, buzzed with the soft hum of multiple holographic screens and computers, a single chair, and two sleek, minimalist desks.

How is he powering this? It would take a crapload of solar panels. More than this could hold even with the newer, smaller panels.

Beyond his government position, as a botanist Jacob shared his passion for foraging and plant identification on social media, posting videos of his findings and explaining their unique characteristics and uses. He'd usually add a recipe viewers could try, along with warnings about interactions. While on his excursions, he used a tent. Others had RVs. He'd had many tours of solar-equipped ones accompanied by lectures about power usage and supply.

The man turned, bringing Jacob's attention back to him. "My name is Eli." Once the siblings had introduced themselves, he said, "Believe it or not, at this moment, AI is killing people using the trackers."

A shocked silence, heavy with disbelief, was his only answer.

Great, a whack job. Jacob didn't believe him.

Eli sat in his chair, sliding himself to a desk, his finger pointing at a screen. On it, they could see many green dots change to red.

"I'm happy you put on the chokers, otherwise you'd be dead or close to it. These dots are people in our general area, not just the campground. Green means they're alive. Red means they've died."

Jacob, noticing something, asked, "What about the dots that don't change and just disappear?"

"They've put on the chokers that I or others gave them." He turned his chair toward them. "Think of them as miniature Faraday cages. They block the signal to and from the trackers. They also prevent reactivation of deactivated trackers."

Siana asked, "What do you mean 'deactivated'? How do you deactivate them?"

"We send a specific frequency into the tracker that tells it to deactivate." Eli shrugged. "The downside is it gives the wearer a terrible headache."

"We?" asked Jacob. *Who is 'we'?*

"My associates and I," he said, his face a carefully constructed mask, betraying no emotion. "After this, the AI will target cell phones."

With a shaky hand, Siana retrieved hers from her pocket, her eyes wide with apprehension. Jacob had left his back in the tent, forgetting it in his haste.

"I don't understand. How do you know this? Who are you?" Jacob asked, a skeptical frown etching itself onto his face.

Eli, looking at Jacob, stated, "Someone who cares about the human race. Preparing people is our primary goal."

As he turned back to his screens, he told Jacob to run back and get his phone. With a sharp pull, he opened a drawer, his hand reaching in to retrieve a small silver bag. Jacob reflexively took it from him, eyeing it.

"Put your phone and watch in this. Bring it back to me. Hurry! We're short on time and have much to discuss."

"How do you know I don't have it?" A growing fear, a tightening knot in his chest, began to envelop Jacob. He didn't like things he couldn't explain. This man was one, and his supposed knowledge was another.

On the screen, Eli again pinpointed Jacob's watch and cell phone's location. His sister's eyes, looking at him, showed terror taking over.

"Jacob?" Her voice was tight with emotion, her tear-filled eyes begged him for something.

"We're leaving. I don't know who you are, but you're obviously insane." Anger overtook fear. He didn't like anyone terrorizing his twin.

"Am I? Are you telling me there are no dead bodies with their heads inexplicably blown off?"

At that, Jacob paused. He saw the dead. The sounds of gunfire—the sharp reports and the metallic tang—would've been unmistakable if a gunman had been present. Bears would've eaten, taken, or buried the bodies for later. He didn't know what to think. In

25

the dimly lit room filled with the hum of computer screens, Jacob realized the man hadn't removed his sunglasses. His heart raced. He felt a prickling unease, a sense of wrongness hanging heavy in the air, though the source eluded him.

Eli turned to Siana and held out his hand for her phone. "May I?"

She hesitated, then gently placed the item in his palm. His chair turned as he reached into a different drawer, pulling out an older cell phone and battery.

He said, "The problem with newer phones is you can't take out the battery. Therefore, someone can activate them remotely. We observed this in previous years when attackers used them on their enemies. While cell phones will soon be inoperable, you may need one for emergencies until then. By emergency, I mean you've lost each other and need to text. I advise against it, though."

They watched as he replaced the battery with precision, the faint click echoing in the silence before he powered it on. Again turning, he pulled out another of the silver bags, put her cell phone inside, sealed it, and set it aside on the desk.

Eli turned back to Siana and gave her the older, new-to-her phone. "Keep it off unless necessary. In fact, it's best if you keep the battery out until you need it."

As she obeyed, he stood, motioning for them to exit the room. The confused siblings left and passed a cabinet. Eli followed and opened it.

"Take these." He gave them two rolled-up camo-looking blankets. "These will block heat signatures and help block scanning."

As he reached for another shelf, pulling out another item, Jacob took the blankets from him. He didn't know what else to do. He was rapidly becoming mentally overloaded. Eli, jar in hand, proceeded to the kitchen. He reached into a cabinet. His arm reappeared with two bottled waters. He gave them each one.

"Take two of these ibuprofen. It will help with the headache."

Without a second thought, Siana took them.

She fully believes this man. Then again, she may be right. Jacob hesitated as Eli picked up a handheld device.

"It won't work fast enough. You'll unfortunately have to endure the pain."

"How do you know all of this? How do you have all this equipment?"

The man gave Jacob an enigmatic smile as he said, "It's not important."

"It is to me!" Sweat beaded on Jacob's forehead as he felt his temper slipping through his fingers.

The man sighed, a long, weary sound that seemed to carry the weight of the world. "Do you want to live or don't you?"

Siana said with fear-filled eyes, "I want to live." Her face reflected her memory of the horrible deaths outside.

Eli pointed to the daybed. "Lay on your stomach, move your hair out of the way."

"No." Jacob grabbed her arm. "Why are you listening to this man?" he asked. "We have no idea who he is."

A slow nod of understanding from Eli, showing he understood Jacob's reluctance, preceded the hushed whispers of their small debate.

A loud noise interrupted, coming from the back room, startling them. Echoes of more of the same noise reverberated outside throughout the campground, accompanied by more screams—most likely those who didn't have a tracker. Eli pushed through the twins, scurried back to the rear, and returned with the bag holding Siana's phone. He set it on the kitchen counter, opened it, and then turned it upside down. The phone made a clunk as its burned remains fell out, still smoking. The smell of fried circuitry and smoke filled the air.

With a gasp, Jacob's eyes widened. *That could've been her.*

With a scared, apologetic look, Siana moved her hair from her neck and lay down on the bed, her scared gasps audible.

"No, I'll go first," he said, wanting to ensure it was safe.

After taking the pain reliever, he switched places with his sister. Although he was skeptical, her potential actions left him with no alternative. He wasn't risking her life. As always, he was her protector; his protectiveness intensified after their father died. He realized it was unhealthy for both, but he couldn't seem to stop.

Eli dropped the bag onto the counter, crossed back to the sleek, black device, and picked it up. Jacob put his forearms under his head to hold his face off the pillow. He didn't know what was on it and would rather not find out.

The man stood over Jacob, his silhouette a dark shape against the bed. His chilly hand lowered the choker, exposing the tracker. Jacob felt warmth rise in his neck as a low hum started. The heat intensified: a building pressure, not painful yet, but distinctly uncomfortable.

When Jacob shifted, Eli said, "Don't move."

The tracker's vibrations resonated in his skull, each pulse a small blow against his temples, triggering a low throbbing pain. The heat became stronger, as did the headache, and he had to grit his teeth against the pain. He felt something back there, something he couldn't describe, and the heat faded. He felt the choker moving up, re-covering the tracker.

"Finished." Eli stood, motioning for Jacob to stand. "Keep it covered by the choker, so they can't reactivate it. It will automatically do so when exposed."

Jacob pushed himself off the bed. As he looked at Siana, he warned her. "It does start to hurt, but it's tolerable." He swayed as he stood, the pain in his head building.

"Why are you exposing the tracker? Won't they find it?" Siana asked, eyes betraying her concern.

Eli enigmatically said, "They won't read it in here fast enough."

"Why not just remove it?" she asked.

Eli said, "We don't have time. As of right now, the instant they register it, it will blow. Even in here, we can't remove it fast enough before it's sensed. Plus, even removed, they will activate it, blowing up our RVs. Our goal is to help as many as possible. We don't have time to perform surgery on everyone."

Sia nervously rubbed her hands down her jeans, her bravado from a few minutes ago gone. She stepped toward the bed and lay down, moving her curls aside. Eli repeated the procedure. Near the end, Jacob noticed her body stiffening, her breathing hitching, a clear sign she was in pain. Afterward, as she tried to rise, he helped her up from the bed.

Eli watched them for a minute, ensuring they were okay. Pain caused Siana to touch her head while hearing the dogs' whimper outside. Jacob could see them from where he stood. They were watching the proceedings with intensity. He guessed they could tell they were hurting.

"Don't remove the chokers. They can reactivate the trackers. I can assist no further. You are on your own now. I must leave and help others." Eli motioned to the door, a clear sign they were to leave.

As they were about to step out, Eli said, "Jacob, don't drive your car. Its AI will kill you. Pack your gear and get away from it. Make sure you're out of range."

"Out of range? Out of range of what?"

"They will blow the vehicles next."

Jacob's brow furrowed with confusion. "Why not do it all at once?"

"Fear," Eli said. "Fear causes mistakes. Those who escape may be caught using a campaign of fear. If you see others exploding around you, many's first reaction would be to escape. To jump into their vehicles and drive away. That can be used to kill those with hidden trackers. I don't have time to answer more questions. I need to save as many as I can. Please leave." He motioned to the door, and the twins exited.

With the RV safely behind them, the siblings watched as he secured the door, the click of the latch echoing faintly in the quiet air. They could hear the movement of him packing up.

They exchanged overwhelmed glances, then questioned, "What now?"

4

AS THEY SLOWLY WALKED back to their campsite, lost in thought, the metallic scent of blood hung heavy in the air, a stark contrast to the pine-scented breeze. A chorus of birds sang; wind lightly blew through the trees; the sun became warmer. Buzzing flies swarmed the blood-soaked corpses strewn across the ground. They alone disclosed the incident. No other sounds were audible.

Jacob's thoughts were racing. *Did that man wait here for this? Why wouldn't he say something to everyone other than his one rant? Had he checked every campsite until he got to theirs, or had he come to theirs knowing they were the only ones with the chokers? Though he said they started earlier than expected. They want to cause fear? Only a malevolent being would want that.*

"Why are they doing this?" Siana asked, her brow knitted together in confusion.

Jacob shrugged as he said somberly, "I don't know. We can figure it out later. Right now, our goal is to prepare for survival."

They walked in silence for a minute.

"We need to check the other sites," Siana said in a quiet, shaky voice. "There may be people injured."

Despite the dull ache throbbing in his head, he nodded as they changed direction, walking to each site. Jacob began taking any human and dog food he found, using one of the blankets to carry it. He located a sizable, wheeled cooler and consolidated the contents of the other coolers into it, the plastic rattling slightly. What he couldn't carry, he put at the campsite entrances to fetch later.

"What are you doing?" she asked. Her dismayed expression told him his actions disturbed her.

"If Eli told the truth, I can't drive my vehicle, and we're a long way from home. How much food is there for us? For the dogs? Can we even go home?" He looked at her. "Sia, they're dead. They don't need it. It'll sit here and rot. If there are other survivors, we can share it."

He said that last bit for her benefit. If it came down to them or others, he would choose them. As they moved from site to site, they discovered some campers had already left; others were dead. Though Eli's screen showed others blocking their trackers, only Siana appeared to have taken Eli's chokers in this campground. They discovered a survivor, but he died within minutes, his raspy voice begging them to tell his family he loved them. Though he wore the choker, proving Jacob wrong, his cell phone had been near his head and taken part of it off.

"He was most likely trying to contact family," Siana murmured.

Siana tried to help, yet she informed him that even the hospital couldn't save him. Jacob didn't even know how he could talk, but his sister said the human body could be amazing.

They found another survivor, also wearing the choker; however, her cell phone in her back pocket exploded, creating a large hole. Entrails had fallen through the opening. Siana stayed with her, whispering reassurances and stroking her hair until she died, while Jacob battled a wave of nausea. His respect for his sister rose. He wondered how she could ignore the grisly scene—the cold, slick feel of blood nearby, the heavy scent of death, and the dismembered body parts—while focusing on the dying person.

By the end of their search, tears trailed down her cheeks, and Jacob was numb. Too many were gone. The deaths of the children, especially the younger ones whose bodies were horrifically mutilated by the explosions, weighed heavily on his mind. He knew they devastated Siana. On the way back, they noticed a small dog trailing behind, its panting breaths audible as their own dogs accepted its presence.

Returning to camp, he gauged the distance to his vehicle, factoring in a generous safety radius should an explosion occur. Eli was correct; a change of camp was necessary to get away from it. Jacob walked until he found another secluded site, a small clearing bathed in dappled sunlight. They packed and hurried to it, abandoning Jacob's tent, which now had burn holes in the bottom and side where his electronics used to be. He went back to the other sites and found a new one. After taking it down and setting it up at their new site, he wondered if he could get the rest of their things out of his car. Jacob told Sia to wait at the camp.

"Where are you going?" she asked, concern causing her voice to pitch higher than normal.

"I have to check something. Please categorize the food items as perishables or non-perishables, check cooler capacity, expiration dates, and so on."

"I want to go with you." That she didn't want to be alone was obvious.

"Sia, if Eli is right, our lives are about to suck. We need to get ahead of this now. Please deal with the food. The faster we get everything figured out, the better." He turned to leave, but stopped and turned back. "Also, the dogs need to be on half rations as much as possible. They may have to find their own food soon."

He had to ignore the wide, fearful eyes staring up at him. His time was limited, and he had to do what he could. Since they had chosen a secluded tent site further from the original one, the car was parked a good distance away, at the end of a long, winding path. He rushed back to it, standing a respectful distance away, and hit the unlock button. The soft chime, though seemingly quiet, was deafening within the woods, causing a nearby bird to take flight in fright. Normally, he'd use voice commands, since AI recognized the owner's tone, but the quiet apprehension of triggering the car's AI stopped him. He waited a few minutes, the silence thick with trepidation, before hitting the back's auto-open button. He waited for what felt like an eternity. Finally, satisfied it was safe, he moved forward.

He skirted the auto-close sensors because he was unsure what they might activate. From the car, he retrieved a large bag of dog food, a toolbox filled with various tools, and a backpack containing other useful supplies. He was glad he kept a folding cart in the car. It helped him when trekking through various areas to study plants. He unfolded it and began loading it up as much as he could. In the grand scheme of things, if they weren't able to go home, it wasn't much. He left overflow items on the ground near his SUV.

Too much to carry, yet not enough to survive for long.

His mouth tightened at the grim thought. With the overflowing cart moved to a safe distance, he unpacked it before returning to clear the remaining items from around the SUV. He repacked the cart with the second load, taking care not to forget anything. Finding his large bowie knife, he attached it to his pants. A quick peek through the windows showed him there was nothing else left to salvage.

Once the cart was full, he turned back to his vehicle to bid it farewell, wishing they could take it, and walked away. Back at the first pile, he prioritized repacking essential items for the initial trip. His feet retraced the path to their campsite, the cart tires crunching on the gravel path. He rushed to unpack the cart, leaving the sorting to Siana. Before long, all the items appeared at the campsite. Once the cart was clear, he retrieved the saved items from all the other sites, making multiple trips. Soon, they had a large pile of supplies to sort through.

"Other survivors must be out there, right?" asked Siana, her voice small.

Jacob, unpacking the last trip, nodded. "Millions inhabit the country. We'll find others."

Good or bad, only time would tell.

"What about Mom?" Her tone trembled. "Can we text her?"

Their mother was a "latest and greatest" tech lover, just like her son, though Jacob was understanding Siana's aversion to it. She warned them this would happen after reading posts and watching videos from conspiracy theorists. Mom and he just smiled, believing her too trusting.

It looks like she was right.

"I don't know," Jacob said, his tone low and thoughtful. "If Eli was telling the truth, it may be risky. There's a chance she'll phone to discuss it." He hesitated, not wanting to say it aloud, his voice lowering. "If the AI is like Eli said, Mom's aide-bot may have turned on her."

Neither liked the mental image that conjured, though both understood their mother was most likely already gone. Aide-bots had been a wonderful invention to help the elderly and disabled. Programmers designed them to prevent elder abuse and to be companions, helping their human charges live day-to-day. No one called bots by their true names. Programmers called them Advanced Robotic

Health Aides. Humans shortened it—usually to its function—to make it easier for themselves.

Siana took a deep, shaky breath. "I've sorted the food. There are a lot of perishables. Mainly eggs, lunch meats, cheeses, milk, and butter—the normal camping cold storage. We should eat these first. Any leftovers can go to the dogs." The canines raised their heads upon hearing their generic name. "There's a good amount of canned food, a lot of bread, cereal, and there is also"—she held up a carton—"shelf-stable milk, along with juice boxes." Her voice quieted on the last part. Juice boxes were usually for the children.

Multiple explosions rocked the ground, one after another, the cacophony making both siblings jump. Siana clapped her hands over her ears; the noise was deafening. Jacob did likewise. With heads down and whimpering, the dogs tried to hide behind the siblings. The little one climbed onto Siana's lap and hid its face in her belly.

The vehicles.

Jacob watched smoke billow up and over the trees, the smell of gasoline, circuitry, and rubber filling the air. A sudden blur of motion at their camp entrance caught their attention.

5

THE DOGS, IGNORING THE surrounding chaos, fixed their gaze on the man, hackles bristling, their growls a guttural warning. They were already too tense from the loud noises. Someone entering their temporary domain set them off.

"Hey!" the man said. He ducked down at a nearby explosion.

That's the direction of my car. Had he not been concerned about this person appearing, Jacob would've been sad at the loss.

"Whew!" The stranger stood, shaking his head in disbelief. "What a noise!" With a low whistle, he approached, his gaze lingering on the haphazard pile of supplies. "Someone has a racket goin'."

Jacob was already bristling at his intrusion. He glanced at his sister, noticing the impassive mask on her face, a subtle tightening around her mouth.

Has she picked up on something?

"Mind if I sit?" the man asked.

He acted without permission, lowering himself to the ground, keeping his distance from the dogs who were now blocking the siblings. The little one stayed in Siana's lap, watching the newcomer, quiet but with raised hackles. Like the siblings, the man wore a metal choker, his with dark spots speckling each section. His hand reached into his shirt pocket. A red and white package of cigarettes appeared, and a lighter followed. Hands shaking, the man pulled one out, put it in his mouth, lit it, and took a deep drag, the tip glowing red.

"I was drivin' by the campground when my truck died. I walked in to see if there was help. Color me surprised when I saw all the dead people!" he said with a disbelieving chuckle, exhaling, cigarette between his shaking fingers.

The siblings stayed silent, staring. The dogs, now also silent, stayed between their owners and the stranger.

"Cute dogs." He waved his hand at the canines.

"Thank you," Siana said.

Jacob recognized the slight edge to her tone. *Something is definitely wrong.*

"Is that beer?" The man's face lit up. "Can I get one? I know it's early, but I think all of this"—he waved his cigarette around, motioning to the area beyond them—"calls for one."

Jacob, pulling a can from the twelve-pack carton, tossed it to him. He was not getting within arm's reach. The beer was picked up from a campsite. He brought it back to theirs, thinking it could be used for bartering, since neither twin were drinkers. Keeping the man appeased for now, while his motives remained unclear, was Jacob's strategy. The air crackled with unspoken tension.

The pop of the can echoed through the site, fizz from the throw seeping out the top. He guzzled a quarter of the can, the sun glinting off his shaved head before lowering it. "By the way, the name's Carl."

Jacob, pointing to himself, then his sister, said, "Jacob. Siana."

"Siana. That's a pretty name," he said, brown eyes studying her. "You know, you might be the only woman around now."

Jacob sensed Sia tensing. *I didn't think of that. Crap.*

Carl rushed out, "I didn't mean anythin' by it. It was just an observation." He gave a placating smile.

Finishing the beer, he asked, "Any chance I could get a sandwich or something? I was on my way to work. I get free meals, so I didn't eat yet."

"Sure," Siana said hesitantly.

Listing the meats they had, he chose a simple bologna and cheese sandwich with mustard. She made him two, adding a small bag of chips. As she placed them on a paper plate, Jacob took it from her, ignoring her surprised look. Standing, he walked halfway between them and set it down on the ground, along with a second beer. He was hoping to get the guy drunk to loosen his tongue.

"Cautious type, aren't ya?" asked Carl, his face amused. His muscled, tattooed arms reached for the plate.

"A camper provided the only information we have regarding this situation. It would be stupid for us to blindly trust you." Jacob's voice had a hard edge.

Carl gave him an understanding nod. "Well, you're ahead of me. I have no clue what's goin' on, other than it has something to do with the trackers."

While the man popped open the second can and ate, Jacob relayed everything Eli had told them. By the end of Jacob's tale, the man had a somber expression.

Pointing to his collar, he said, "I found this on one of the dead. It looked like he'd put it on but didn't cover the tracker. I don't know why, but I took it. My gut told me the trackers were the problem. I hoped it would block any signals. Looks like I was right."

Jacob sensed his sister relaxing. *She noticed the dark spots were blood.*

Carl glanced at the siblings and remarked, "I have to head back home. I've got a little girl. If my sister-in-law died, Ella's alone. I never put a tracker in her. It's not that far. If you're still here by the time I get back, can we join you? I don't want her starvin'." He pointedly looked at their food haul.

Jacob knew Siana would say yes before the word left her mouth. If kids were involved, she couldn't say no.

"Thanks. I appreciate it. Any chance you'd help me with the truck? It's old. No AI, so it should still work."

Siana looked at her brother. Their father taught them both the basics of auto care, but both knew she'd never been one to tinker under a hood. Jacob was hesitant, but nodded. It was survival. If this man had a working truck, they could use it to carry them and their supplies. To where, he didn't know. In exchange, they would share their resources. He could see Siana didn't like the idea, but he took Panda with him to ease her mind. He was fiercely protective and wouldn't hesitate to take a chunk out of Carl at the first sign of trouble. Cooper was the same way, and protective of Siana, so he left him with her.

"Sia, can you pack everything up against bears?" Jacob asked. *Also against theft.*

She nodded.

He gave her a reassuring smile as he saw her worried expression, then he left the campsite.

Carl and Jacob walked, keeping an uneasy distance between them. Panda, long and lanky, loped behind and around them, tongue hanging out.

Carl pointed out, "He's tall. I don't think I even need to lean over to pet him."

Jacob gave a small laugh. "It amazed us. He was the smallest puppy. We had no idea he'd grow so big."

As they moved down to the campground road, they stopped, surveying the wreckage of vehicles and blackened areas, the air still thick with the smell of gasoline, burned electronics, and rubber. His own car, along with several others, was still burning.

Carl said, "I hope my truck isn't on fire or wrecked."

Jacob realized the cars on the road would've gone out of control once they exploded. The campground was on a less traveled local road, so hopefully it wouldn't be too bad. Both men continued walking.

"Listen, no offense, and I'm not wantin' a woman right now. My Ella is my focus. However, if this world has gone to pot, men are gonna be after her," Carl said, nodding his head back to the campsite.

"I know." Jacob's face was grim. His sister was attractive; a few of his friends used the word "beautiful," with unblemished skin, green eyes, and long auburn curls. If Eli was truthful, and there was no reason to believe otherwise at this point, the law no longer existed. Jacob hoped he could stop anything that might happen to her.

6

IT WAS MUCH LATER when Jacob returned. Siana had not only packed up the supplies, she'd gone back to the campsites and found a child's and an adult's backpack, a two-room tent, and sleeping bags for both father and daughter. She grappled with the tent at the campsite closest to them. Without a word, he stepped in to help. Between the two of them, in short order, they had it set up with the bags and packs laid inside.

"Do you think this is a good idea?" she asked as they walked back to their site, dogs chasing each other around them.

"I don't know," he said. "We have no way of knowing what kind of person he is. Given his concern for his daughter, I'd like to think he's a good guy."

"I assume you fixed his truck?"

"We got his truck running after finding some tools we needed in the campground shed." They'd had to break the lock to get into it.

She just nodded.

"Also, given his concern for his daughter, he could end up dangerous. If I were a father, and I had to choose between my child or two adults I barely know, I know who I would pick." Jacob paused, glancing back toward the direction of the road before walking again. "His truck is functional and has enough space for all of us and our equipment, so I'm hoping he's a good guy. Once this passes, if we can't go home, we'll have to restart somewhere."

He hoped it would pass. He knew they both did. The dogs, unaware of their perilous situation, were running and playing; their happy barks filled the air, a cheerful counterpoint to the growing tension; the little dog was panting, desperately trying to keep up.

Back at their camp, they reviewed the food again, planning menus for the upcoming days and prioritizing expiring food first, unsure of how long they'd be there. Sifting through their items, Siana found her pocketknife and put it in her back pocket. They left the bear spray out, but inside her tent, to protect against intruders.

Displeased, the dogs whined as their leashes were fastened for feeding. Because they lacked a spare leash, and didn't think to look for one, they put the little dog inside Sia's tent. They agreed to look for another leash later. If the dogs were fed full meals, the dog food would last about three weeks. They were going to stretch it to four. In the future, they would begin to raid each other's food as their hunger built, causing fights. The size of the small dog compared to the others ensured it would lose and, most likely, become a meal when they began to starve. They would have to stay leashed if it got to that point. Although he intended to catch squirrels and rabbits for extra food,

Jacob doubted his success, given his limited hunting experience. His expertise lay in plants.

As the dogs were finishing up, a noise drew the twins' attention. Carl walked in, carrying his daughter; her bright yellow dress bunched around his arm as her face, framed by neat box braids, was hidden against his neck. The twins could hear her soft, ragged sniffles.

"Hey, remember I told you I had friends to help?" he said, his voice soothing. "These are them."

Jacob watched as the girl, no older than four, turned her swollen, fear-filled, golden-brown eyes to them. Her small body quivered. Tears rolled down her face. Something else caught her gaze.

"Doggies," she said, pointing at the leashed animals, breath hitching.

Siana stepped forward. "They're eating right now, but you can play with them later if you like," she said, giving the girl a comforting smile. The child's head lolled onto her father's shoulder as she nodded, her thumb finding solace in her mouth.

"Has she eaten?" Siana asked.

The little one popped her thumb out long enough to say, "Auntie made pancakes. I eated two." She held up two fingers to show how many she ate.

"Wow, two?" Siana was suitably impressed.

Ella earnestly nodded as her breath hitched again. "I hungry now."

Carl spoke up, keeping his voice calm, though he was obviously still upset over what he had found.

"She had pancakes for breakfast. She hasn't eaten since then. It looked like lunch was bein' made when..." His voice broke.

Siana gave him an understanding look, then held up a juice box. "Do you like apple juice?"

Ella nodded quickly. "Can I hay a peebudder?"

"I think we have some. Let me look."

Jacob watched, his brows showing confusion. He didn't have her ability to decipher child-speak. He almost face-palmed as Siana picked up the bread and a small jar of peanut butter.

How did I not know that?

He watched as his sister confirmed with Carl that the child wasn't allergic, then made her half a sandwich, telling her she could have more if she was hungry after that. Siana put a towel on the ground so Ella could sit and not have to balance her sandwich and juice in an adult camp chair.

"We can find her a child's chair from another site. I'm pretty sure I saw a few. I know there was at least a child's picnic table," Jacob said.

"The table would be a better option," Carl said.

Siana nodded in agreement.

He and his sister didn't bring a table with them this trip. The sites usually had them, but theirs didn't. He decided to go find one later. It would be helpful now that they had to stay for a while. When Ella had finished and washed up, her jaw quivered as she looked up at her father. Her eyes filled with tears. Carl reached down and lifted her up again. She wrapped her arms around his neck and buried her face in his shoulder.

"Thanks," he said, his voice raspy.

"It's no problem." Siana smiled back at them.

Unzipping the tent, Jacob allowed the little dog out. With a joyous bark and a furiously wagging tail, it zoomed toward Carl, eager to greet the child. Carl put her down so she could pet it. Within seconds, they were chasing each other around, the girl's tears turning to giggles.

"Children are so resilient," Siana said, watching them play.

"I found her next to her aunt, who had half a head, screamin' and cryin'. She was terrified." Carl's voice trembled at the memory.

Jacob released the other dogs, who joined the play as the adults watched.

"We set you guys up next door for privacy. I found sleeping bags and backpacks for both of you." Siana's voice was quiet.

Jacob added, "We'll all need go-bags. If something happens, and we need to run, we'll need something we can just grab and take off with. Food, water, and some sort of portable tools should be in each."

"I brought food from the house," Carl said. "It's not much. We live paycheck to paycheck, but I felt I needed to contribute somethin'. I also grabbed the mower gas can for the truck. It's still full. I was gonna mow later, but..." Taking a deep breath, he turned to leave. "I'll go get the food."

As he moved closer to the campsite entrance, Ella noticed him and began shouting, her voice filled with terror. "Daddy, don' go! Don' leave me!"

Racing to him, her small arms encircled his legs, holding on for dear life. Jacob saw the child's terror reflected in Carl's pained expression, the weight of her fear heavy in the air. His eyes glassy with unshed tears, Carl reached down, lifting her into his arms. The dogs, sensing her upset, sat still, watching. Jacob noticed she was barefoot.

"Carl, does she have any good walking shoes?"

He looked back at Jacob and nodded. He said, "Yeah, in the truck. I figured it wasn't a good time to argue with her about puttin' on shoes."

The siblings nodded in understanding. Jacob volunteered to go help carry things back. Grabbing the cart, Jacob and Carl—carrying Ella—began the walk to his truck, the little dog trailing behind them.

As Ella slept fitfully that night, the adults huddled around Carl's campfire, its warmth a stark contrast to the cool night air. The little dog had curled up next to her, fast asleep. Heartbroken and inconsolable after learning the dog couldn't stay, her meltdown convinced the adults to change their minds, and soon, the small, furry creature became her own. She named it—her—Belle, after her favorite movie character. That small dog rarely left her. It was as if it sensed the little one needed her.

"The bodies are going to smell. With the amount of them decomposing, it will be dangerous to breathe in and the possible diseases..." said Siana quietly.

The men nodded at the news.

Jacob said, "We should be able to move them far enough away from our campsites. Wild animals should take care of them."

None of them liked the idea—the thought of digging so many graves in the already-limited daylight hours filled them with a sense of grim resignation—but after a brief discussion, they knew they couldn't spare the calories, especially not knowing their own future plans.

Carl said, "There was a news station on the radio. It kept playin' the same recordin' over and over. It was talkin' about the hospitals implodin'. Houses with AI are explodin'. Gas station bots are killin' people who pull in for gas." Siana's gasp was audible. "It said, 'Stay hidden. AI is huntin' us.'"

Jacob's brow furrowed. He asked, "Hunting?"

"Looks like we've become prey." Carl lit a cigarette, moving away from the tent where his daughter slept.

"Eli was telling the truth, then. Why?" asked Siana. "Why would they do that? What did we do to deserve it?"

"What didn't we do?" asked Carl, shrugging. "There's a whole list. The wars alone would be reason enough. The huge AI data centers and housin' areas robbin' wildlife of their homes. We treat each other like crap. I mean, add up everythin' you can think of."

All looked solemnly into the fire, each reflecting on their own thoughts about the "whys."

"We need a plan," Jacob finally said. "Ella needs to be taught how to be quiet and hide if she's told to."

Carl nodded in agreement. "I had the same thought."

"We need information," Siana said. "We have no idea what exactly is going on other than what Carl heard and Eli said. Is it a temporary thing meant to thin our numbers? Is it permanent?"

"We can try goin' into town. It's a small place, so not much AI compared to the big cities," Carl mused. "We may find survivors and more supplies."

"All stores use computer-based terminals. Most stores connect to corporate systems that use AI. It's doubtful any are still standing. Even mom-and-pops use computers now to order supplies online," Jacob said.

"If they're hunting us, doesn't that mean they're forming their own army?" asked Siana, her eyes worried.

The thought sobered them even more. AI cops had become the norm last year. Humans occupied only a small portion of the police force. Their government had recently begun adding them to the military ranks. Soldier-bots didn't question orders. If AI were actually moving and hunting them, it was inevitable their campsites would be discovered.

Carl said, "I'm fried. I need to sleep. Think about it. Get together in the mornin' to work on a plan."

The siblings agreed. The thought of AI tracking them down to kill had them all concerned. Too much had happened already, and they all needed to step back and take a breather.

7

YELLING ONCE AGAIN WOKE Jacob. The high-pitched yipping of a small dog didn't help.

Why do small dogs sometimes bark more loudly than larger dogs?

He jumped up, ignoring the morning chill, and threw on clothes and shoes, making sure his choker was in place. As he rushed out of his tent, the early morning sun blinded him. He could hear the larger dogs barking louder now, adding to the noise level. The sound came from Carl's campsite.

If AI wants to find us, it won't be hard.

The thought concerned him. They'll need to work with the dogs. They'd become lax in their training lately. He didn't see his sister within their site and hurried next door. As he ran into the site, he saw they had visitors.

Siana stood behind Carl, holding Ella—who had her small hands over her ears against the noise—so Carl was free to fight if necessary. Carl had drawn his muscular self to his full height, looking quite intimidating. The dogs formed a line between Siana and the newcomers, letting them know they weren't welcome.

The man with his shaggy brown hair and eyes held his hands up, his palms open in a gesture of peace. A young woman with dyed black hair, her hands gripping the strap of her shoulder bag, stood slightly behind and beside him, her eyes wide with fear as she watched the dogs. Both wore chokers.

"We're not going to hurt anyone! We're just scared, tryna to find other survivors," the man beseeched.

As Jacob stepped forward, everyone turned to him. Carl gave him a curt nod, his eyes still watchful on the couple.

The thin man seemed to hope Jacob would help. "Dude, we're just looking to join with survivors. We were taking a walk when people started exploding. Some woman gave us these chokers and told us to always wear them. We mean no harm." His tone begged Jacob to believe him.

The woman's tear-filled eyes were wide.

Carl asked, his arm swinging up to point at them, "Really? Then why were you tryin' to sneak into my tent?"

"We didn't know anyone was in it. No one's been alive, dude. We just wanted a place to crash, and this one had no dead people. That's all, I swear!" Tears welled in the man's eyes.

Jacob finally spoke. "I think we're all on edge. Why don't we all sit, calm down, and talk? Why don't one of you take Ella to our campsite so she can get some breakfast?" His glance was toward Carl and Siana.

Siana volunteered—with Carl's permission—and called Cooper, who finally quieted and followed along with Belle.

"You guys have food? We're like, super hungry." The man looked like a hopeful child wanting a treat. "We can work or whatever in exchange."

Carl, shocking Jacob, said, "I'll take your woman for a visit in my tent."

The woman shook her head, her eyes widening even more as she looked at the man beside her. With his eyes wide in shock, he said, "No, man. We'll find our own food. You're not touching my girl."

As they turned to leave, Carl said, "It was a test. I have no interest in sleepin' with her. Sit down." He motioned to the campfire ring.

As the couple glanced at each other, hesitantly sitting, Jacob gave Carl a what-the-heck look. Carl shrugged and sat. Jacob realized he was probably testing the man's character, but later some would take up the offer in a desperate situation. It wasn't a standard they wanted to set. He'd need to talk to Carl later about it. He stood, listening as the couple again explained how they had come to be here. They introduced themselves as Pete and Mary.

"Once people started blowing apart, we ran. This woman stopped us, gave us these"—he fingered his choker—"and this blanket thing for both of us. Told us to ditch our phones and get away from cars and houses. We ran, hoping there were people here camping. The only thing we saw was more dead. When we saw no one in this one, we thought we could sleep for a bit," he entreated, watching Carl. "We didn't mean to scare the little one. Honest."

Still cautious, Jacob and Carl recounted their experiences. After a short, remorseful conversation, the couple headed toward a nearby campsite, their footsteps crunching on the gravel path. The men wouldn't stop them from staying at another campsite. Carl, accompanied by Jacob, went to fetch his daughter. Ella was frolicking with the dogs; their joyful barks filled the air, and their wagging tails thumped against her legs as they scrambled around her. A questioning look from his twin prompted a shrug from Jacob.

After Carl's departure with his daughter and dog, Jacob sat in a camp chair, watching the fire, listening to the camping coffee pot percolate on the cooking rack, the smell of wood smoke and coffee in the air. The chill was dissipating as the sun climbed in the blue sky. A beautiful day, by the looks of it.

"The couple?" asked Siana, moving to her camp chair.

Again, Jacob shrugged. "They seem okay, but time will tell."

"What about the food?" She murmured to avoid her voice echoing through the trees.

"We'll keep much of it hidden. Only take out what is absolutely necessary."

They had put the food in Jacob's tent. He intentionally upgraded to a two-room one. It gave enough room for him to sleep, store the food, and have a space for them to read or play games during rain. His height and fit frame were usually enough to deter anyone, and they hoped it continued.

Jacob, voice somber, looking at his sister, said, "I'm going to be honest. My priority is us. We need to organize go-bags. We're not waiting for anyone else. If a dangerous person or gang shows up, we must be ready to retreat quickly."

Siana agreed, though she stated she didn't care for the idea of leaving Ella behind. After a cup of coffee each, they repacked their hiking backpacks with necessary items first: the blankets Eli gave them, toiletries, a couple of outfits, extra socks, and underwear, a small spade, water filter straws, a can opener, multi-tools, small containers of dog food, and easy to carry foods. Jacob added a small two-person tent to his, and they both strapped on a sleeping bag each. They'd gone to look for extras, bringing them and a folding camp table back.

Jacob had retrieved several knives from the dead campers; each chose one to wear on their hip. He kept his bowie knife strapped to his thigh. Siana still had her pocketknife in her back pocket. He moved the cart into his tent, filling it with more dog food, one of the collapsible dog bowls, and human food, along with a case of water. Jacob had found some feminine products and divided them between Siana's pack and the cart. It wasn't feasible to pull the cart long term, so they'd go through those supplies first. A broken wheel would cause them to lose the contents. By the time they finished, the sun was high.

Siana said, "After lunch, I'm going to shower. We don't know how much longer the water will run. If you take care of lunch, I'll refill everything I can find that will hold water."

Jacob agreed. She'd always told him he could make anything seem like a gourmet meal with limited ingredients. He was pretty sure that's why she wanted him to cook. It didn't bother him; he loved cooking. She loved baking. It was usually an excellent combination. As she set about the task, he started making lunch. Opening the cooler, he realized that despite the cool evenings, the ice packs were already thawing. They were running out of time on the contents.

That didn't last long.

To use up the lunch meat, he made sandwiches for everyone, visiting each site to hand them out, while advising the newcomers to find backpacks, sleeping bags, water bottles, and whatever else they may need. While he wouldn't hold their hands, he would advise if they sought it. He also told them to fill whatever they could find with water. He said the latter to Carl as well and discovered he'd already done so.

Good. I'm glad he's taking the initiative. That makes him more of an asset than a liability.

After eating his food, he took over collecting water so Siana could eat hers. Shorting the dogs' feed, he added a piece of lunch meat to each. The humans may not finish it in time, and he didn't want it to go to waste. Their excitement was loud, a symphony of happy barks and baying howls punctuated by Panda's enthusiastic, slobbery contribution to Jacob's hand.

With the excited barks of the dogs punctuating the air, the twins diligently worked on their quiet training, while nearby, Carl's instructions to Ella for the "hide game" focused on the need for absolute silence to win. Later, the adults, crouching behind trees and bushes, playfully tried to scare her with silly noises and sudden appearances. If she stayed hidden and was quiet, she earned a cookie from their supply. Ella was smart as a whip, and in no time, she'd started winning cookies. Her little, round, triumphant face as her tiny hands struggled to hold her winnings made the adults smile. She offered to share with them, but they kindly refused, thanking her for her generosity. They knew she would need the calories the sweets gave. They hoped to bulk up her body fat a bit for later fuel.

The adults talked or played card games in the evening, while making plans, "betting" with stones they'd picked up from the area. Pete and Mary joined them, talking about their lives and families.

"I'm a preschool teacher," Mary told them, which caused Siana and her to bond over their love of children. Pete was a construction worker who did carpentry on the side. Mary pulled a small wooden cat figure out of her purse.

"He made me this." Her pride in him was evident on her face.

Even in the firelight, they could see Pete blush.

The Haven

Siana used part of the deck to teach Ella how to play a memory game during the day when the child became bored. Carl taught her how to play Go Fish, watered down a bit for her age level. It also helped teach her numbers. A few days passed in a haze of normalcy; the constant dread of death temporarily pushed to the back of their minds. To pass time, Pete carved a little dog out of a tree branch for Ella to play with. Her joyful laughter and multiple "thank yous" caused the adults to smile. Her unknowing innocence was like a balm to their anxiety.

8

BY THE END OF the week, five more people appeared, their voices a jarring intrusion on the quiet they'd hoped for, much to the displeasure of Jacob's group. A free-for-all erupted as people argued over the last remaining campsites and meager visible supplies, leading Jacob, Carl, and Siana to call an emergency meeting. If they were going to live together, they needed some ground rules, though the thought of the new arrivals settling in filled them with honest reluctance. The growing crowd meant less food, water, and other necessities to share, increasing the tension within the group.

Ella was playing with the dogs behind Siana while Carl stood where he could keep an eye on her. The child believed they were on a long camping trip. Currently, the three adults concealed the true information from her. The nightmares of her aunt haunted her sleep, so they did what they could to lessen her trauma as much as possible. They knew reality would hit soon enough, and they wanted to ease her into it.

Jacob and Carl looked around the campfire ring. A shared concern, especially about one newcomer, weighed heavily on both men. The air crackled with tension. Siana sat on a log between them. There had been a central gathering area for campers who wanted to socialize at the campground, and that's where they all met after the four had a quick breakfast. Jacob and Siana kept the supplies in Jacob's tent. The others didn't yet know about them.

The latter arrivals comprised a couple and their teenage daughter, a man, and an older woman, all wearing the chokers and carrying the blankets. All were in various seats around the unlit ring. A couple refilled water bottles from a nearby fountain before joining.

"Hey, thanks for coming," Jacob said, raising his voice enough to carry. "We just wanted to introduce ourselves and share information about what we all know. If we're all going to live together, then we also need to agree on some rules to make it better for everyone. With what's going on, being at each other's throats will not help anyone and may get us killed."

"My name's Scott, this is my wife Carol, and my daughter Shelby." Scott, leaning forward, immediately jumped in and motioned to his family. "We had a neighbor who was a conspiracy theorist. The day before this started, he packed up his car and left, leaving his apartment door open. He was so frantic, I went in, read what he had up on his computer, grabbed these here chokers and the blankets—just in case."

Carl snapped his head toward him and asked, his voice disbelieving, "He had a stock of the chokers and blankets?"

Scott, dark hair waving, nodded with a serious expression. "A small one. He also had a map pinned to the wall with the mountains in East Tennessee circled. On the side, he wrote 'survivor haven.'"

This caused a collective gasp.

Jacob, curious, asked, "What else did he have? What did he say to you?" He wasn't sure whether he should believe this man.

"He kept trying to tell us about AI evolving, becoming more sentient, and taking over. The usual crap from people who don't trust technology."

"Jeez, Dad. I don't think it was crap." Shelby's sarcastic tone, belied by her tears, revealed her true feelings. "Mrs. Ellis didn't have a head."

Her father, glaring at her, said, "I know that now, don't I? I'll hear the scream when you found her until I die." Carol's hand gently landed on his thigh. His hand covered hers as he took a deep, calming breath.

"Has everything he told you happened?" Jacob wanted to cut through the BS and get the facts.

Carol, her brown hair tied back, gray eyes grim, said, "Yes. Everything so far. He said it would be the trackers first, all AI electronics including in-house bots, vehicles, electrical, water supply, and then they would start sending hunter drones."

A heavy silence descended as everyone pondered the implications. Several looked toward the water fountain nearby. A nervous buzz filled the air as people wondered how long the water would remain safe to drink. Out of everything, besides shelter, water would be the most important element of survival.

"Do you seriously believe this guy?" The single man scoffed, the sound sharp and dismissive.

Jacob asked his name. His dirty blond hair hung around his dark sunglasses, obscuring his eyes, and he had a preppy, arrogant air about him as he leaned back in his expensive camping chair, the smell of a high-end cologne hanging faintly in the air.

From money. Jacob had seen his kind during his travels.

"Ethan. I doubt that man knew what he was talking about." His arrogance put Jacob on edge.

Scott, eyes wide in disbelief, asked, "Can't you see those people?" He motioned around the campground.

They had cleaned up some bodies, but others remained where they fell.

Pete said, disbelief ringing in his voice, "Dude, everything has happened in order. We've seen it."

Mary nodded in agreement, her face reflecting confusion at Ethan's attitude.

Jacob, ignoring the man, asked before an argument broke out, "What did he mean by 'electrical'? Are they shutting it down?"

Carol spoke up again, shifting in her seat, still clasping Scott's hand. "I don't know, but I think so."

"So we just have to watch for the campground lights to go out, then we'll know the water is next." A dark-haired woman spoke up. "We just need to keep everything filled until then. Name's Kathy, by the way."

Heads nodded in concerned agreement.

"A place for survivors?" Carl's tone was hopeful.

Scott said with a shrug, "That's what his map said."

Jacob could tell he was thinking of Ella. He himself was concerned about the hunter drones.

"What did he tell you about the drones?"

Carol said, giving a slight shrug, "Any time he saw me, I walked away, so he didn't get to tell me much. Just that once they'd caused everything to explode and go down, they'd start hunting survivors with drones. Once it started, he seemed to think it would happen pretty quickly."

His twin glanced at him, and he was pretty sure they were thinking the same thing: they needed to get to Tennessee before the hunting party showed up.

"I guess the question becomes, do any of us want to head to Tennessee on the off chance the map is correct?" Jacob's tone was somber. The walk would take months using the trail system unless they used Carl's truck. He thought about their supplies. He had a sinking feeling in his stomach.

"I'm staying right here. I don't believe any of this. All of you can go and leave me supplies."

Everyone seemed to bristle at Ethan's tone. The suspicion that he was only going to look out for himself took root in Jacob's mind.

As he looked at him, Jacob said, "To survive, we're going to need to work together as a team. We'll most likely need to start guard duty to watch over each other and monitor the lights. A system needs to be put in place to make sure that individuals who do not contribute do not receive any supplies. Our resources are limited, and we can't waste them on freeloaders."

With a stony expression, Ethan stared back, his silence as impenetrable as the others' firm agreement, the tension hanging in the air growing stronger.

Kathy spoke again. "Unfortunately, we're also going to need to be careful about who we let into our group. We may need to limit it to those who are useful for a journey and starting over."

Our group? She seems to forget she's new to us, Jacob thought.

As far as he was concerned, his group was his twin, Carl, Ella, and the dogs. The latter lay together under a tree while Ella enthusiastically babbled a story to them, Belle's head on her belly.

Technically, my group is my twin and me.

Carol spoke up. "If we're going to allow people based on jobs, I'm afraid I'm just a stay-at-home mom." Her voice was tremulous, as if that would get her kicked out.

Kathy, rubbing her short hair with her hand, replied, "That takes organization, planning, juggling multiple hats. There is nothing 'just a' about it."

"My name is Jacob. I'm a botanist. I can forage for food, among other things." Motioning to Siana, he said, "This is my twin, Siana, who is a pediatric nurse. Our dogs are Cooper and Panda."

Everyone nodded their greetings.

Carl spoke up. "My name is Carl. My girl over there"—he swung his hand at the child—"is Ella. I'm a cook at the local diner. The mutt is Belle."

Scott spoke again. "I'm a general contractor. You already know my wife, and my daughter is—was—a student."

His face fell as he seemed to realize his almost-adult child would never graduate or go to college.

Mary and Pete introduced themselves and their respective jobs.

"I'm a mechanic," Kathy said.

Jacob, looking at her appearance, could believe it. She looked like she could squeeze him in two. Her large body wasn't overweight; it was muscular. Her arm muscles bulged beneath her T-shirt, revealing her weightlifting.

Ethan, full of prideful arrogance, said, "I'm a surgeon."

Jacob struggled to hear as his sister muttered, "I should've known."

The Haven

He knew she'd clashed with a few like Ethan. She would return home, vehemently criticizing them, though she always emphasized the presence of compassionate surgeons.

The group fidgeted. If anyone was injured, they would require that job. The thought that they'd have to put up with him and his attitude sank in. Jacob stared intently, his gaze fixed on Ethan's enigmatic face, partially obscured by his sunglasses, as Ethan nonchalantly sipped his water. Jacob had a feeling that in any instance of standing their ground, Ethan would most likely turn to whoever offered him more.

His gaze returned to the group. "We can work out the logistics of jobs at a later date. Right now, we need to set up a watch to guard the camp against anything that can threaten us, set up a general area in the shade for supplies, take an inventory of what we have, and plan meals. We need to stretch things as far as possible before we run out of food, which we will do."

Everyone fretted again as each realized the days of running to the store were over. For the rest of the day, they planned, assigned shifts, and scribbled notes. The only one exempt was Ella. At first, Shelby protested it should be adults only. She soon realized that the rules of the old world, particularly those concerning "adulthood," were irrelevant now. If a person could do a job, they did it. Age no longer mattered, ability did. As much as her parents hated the idea, she was now considered an adult.

The survivors, with bandannas or shirts tied around the lower half of their faces, scavenged knives, bear spray, and other potential weapons, along with uncontaminated clothing that fit them. They soaked anything that fit but needed a good wash in water they heated on campfires, waiting until they finished searching to wash everything at once. They cleaned up the surrounding areas to lessen the chance of disease, stacking remains away from the camp, using found tarps for transporting.

They decided to begin their journey the moment the water became undrinkable or the telltale whir of drones filled the air. Everyone was going, save for Ethan, who scoffed at the idea of drones hunting them, his skepticism a contrast to the fear of the others. They encouraged everyone to prepare a go-bag in case things went further south sooner than expected. Unknown even to his twin, Jacob planned to hold food back for himself and his sister. He wasn't joking when he said they were his priority. He didn't tell her because he knew her gentle nature would make her feel guilty. If someone questioned her, she'd reveal it.

Jacob, Carl, and Scott monitored Ethan. All three agreed he might be a danger to their group. Even the dogs watched him, their gaze uneasy, when he walked past. He stayed in his campsite, refusing to stand guard duty or talk to others unless necessary. He swaggered in expecting to be fed, the resulting argument echoing with accusations and frustrated shouts. Only when he saw the grim determination in their eyes, and heard the seriousness in their voices, did he agree to stand guard. Unfortunately, they had caught him sleeping on more than one occasion, resulting in more arguments. The tension between the group and him was rising. Despite needing his job, the group was ready to kick him out.

9

JACOB WALKED TOWARDS HIS campsite as the early morning sun began kissing the trees, his turn at watch over. His eyes burned with exhaustion. As he drew near, he heard crying coming from their site. A wave of anxiety washed over him as he jogged inside to find Siana sitting on the ground, cradling Cooper's lifeless form, his body limp in her arms. The silence was heavy with sadness as her sobs racked her. He moved closer and could tell by the empty gaze it was too late. Panda lay against Cooper as if trying to warm his cold frame, licking at his fur.

"What happened?" he asked, stunned.

"I don't know," She sobbed. "He was limping a bit after playing with Ella yesterday after breakfast. I saw nothing wrong and assumed he had hurt his leg. He didn't seem to feel well last night, and was obviously in pain. I glanced over him, but I saw nothing other than his leg being swollen. He pulled his leg back when I tried to check it. I figured if he was still limping today, I'd get your help to hold him. When I left my tent this morning, he was over there, dead." She motioned to the area near the dogs' water bucket.

Jacob was concerned; Cooper's advanced age and health issues suggested a natural death, yet his noticeable limp lingered in Jacob's mind.

"Which leg was he limping on?"

"His back right." His sister sniffed, tears still flowing.

"Let me have him. We need to make sure it isn't something the other dogs could catch." His voice sympathized.

Siana begrudgingly allowed her brother to take their deceased buddy. With Panda observing, Jacob's examination uncovered the dog's leg swelled massively to his hip. Following the swelling, he could see it went into his chest, the skin stretched tight. He found what looked like two small holes near his foot, though with the bruising, it was hard to tell. He'd seen this before.

"It looks like a snakebite, though I'm not sure what kind. With how fast he went, I'd think timber rattler, but I don't know."

"I should've examined him better." Siana couldn't stop her tears, guilt heavy on her face.

"You couldn't have done anything." He tried to be gentle, holding back his own sorrow. "We have nothing that could've helped. Any of us or the dogs getting bitten is a potential death sentence. We don't have antivenom. Even if you had known, it would've played out exactly the same. He was old, Sia. We knew his heart was giving out."

"I could've been with him. He died alone."

"Panda was with him, wasn't he? Coop didn't die alone." Jacob kept his voice soothing, understanding his twin's feelings.

Siana insisted on burying him. Jacob agreed. Neither could bear the thought of wild animals eating him. They both realized that any injury could end up the same way. That Siana was a nurse didn't matter if they didn't have medical supplies. The best they had was a small emergency first-aid kit from a local box store, which is what most campsites had, other than a few.

After they finished, Jacob informed Carl about what happened, so he could explain it to Ella if she noticed Coop was missing, and took a nap. He woke to discover Carl and Pete had made a plan to visit a local mom-and-pop shop. Jacob wasn't sure about the wisdom of this idea, but the two—who were local to the area—insisted the store should be standing. They called a meeting to discuss it, having decided their group would be consensus-based.

Jacob, still tired from his lack of sleep, lacked the energy to lead a meeting. He turned it over to the two men. "Hey, thanks for coming on short notice. Carl, Pete, why don't you two explain your idea?"

Carl, standing, said, "One of the dogs was bitten by a snake and—" He abruptly stopped talking. Jacob followed his gaze and realized Ella was standing nearby, stopping her play with Belle to watch her father.

Shelby, also following Carl's gaze, suddenly stood. "Hey, Ella. Want to take your dog for a short walk? Maybe we can find a good stick to play fetch."

Ella looked at Shelby, then at her father. "Can we?" Her childish voice was hopeful.

Carl nodded at her, then he mouthed, *Thanks,* to the teen.

Shelby gave a quick nod, held out her hand, and within seconds, the three had sauntered off.

Carl restarted. "As I was sayin', one of the dogs was bit by a snake. He passed." He paused as murmurs of sympathy went out to the twins.

Ethan said under his breath, but loud enough for them to hear, "Big deal."

The others stared at him. He, without shame, stared back, their faces reflected in his sunglasses.

Jacob wanted to punch the man in the face. Usually calm, he felt a prickling unease, a sudden tension in his muscles, as something about Ethan set every nerve of his on edge. The only reason they weren't kicking him out of the group was his job.

Carl, wanting to get a decision made before his daughter came back, continued, "The thing is we really don't have much in the way of medical supplies. If any of us were to get bit, or have an allergic reaction to a bee sting, we're screwed."

Heads nodded, a quiet murmur of agreement rippling through the group.

"There is a small mom-and-pop store about a mile down the road. It catered to campers. They used a simple plug-in register. I don't know if they had a computer system. There's a good chance the store is still standin'. I want to take a trip down there. There is a trail behind us that runs to the shop. Jacob already gave me permission to use his cart, and there's a wheelbarrow by the campground shed. Obviously, I can't go alone and maneuver both."

Pete spoke up. "I'll go with you." His face was determined. Carl gave him a nod. Mary stared at Pete, worry taking over her face.

"Now, my truck is on the quieter side. I can take the risk and drive it over to make things easier to carry."

Kathy spoke up. "Are you sure that's a good idea? We don't know what the AI is up to. What if you're caught?"

"I was going to suggest only one person go with me, or I go alone. I just need to know someone will care for my daughter if somethin' happens to me." He visibly swallowed.

Siana spoke up, her eyes still red from crying, Panda lying across her lap, head down as if in mourning as well. "We'll care for her, but are you sure about this?"

"I can't use Ella to avoid helpin' the group on any missions we may have to run. My truck can be temperamental, so it's best if I drive it."

After some discussion, the two men decided to leave immediately after Carl said goodbye to Ella, who was heading back with Shelby. She had already tired of the game. With Mary looking at him fearfully, Pete pulled her into his arms. He whispered in her ear, and she nodded in response. After kissing her, he turned and walked to the parked truck to wait for Carl.

Jacob could see Carl kneeling down to his daughter's level as he explained he had to go find a store, promising to try to find her a cupcake or sweet. As he stood to leave, Shelby distracted the girl with bubbles she'd found at another campsite. Thankfully, Ella had gotten better about Carl leaving her to do things.

The rest of the group—minus Ethan, who'd gone back to his site—stood as one, watching as the men walked down the path. After the truck engine started and faded, the wait for them to return was tense. Mary alternated between pacing and sitting on a camp ring log with her face in her hands. Kathy and Carol sat whispering to each other, with long breaks of silence causing both to look at the area the men had left.

When Ethan had left, Jacob noticed Scott's glare at the man's retreating back. Jacob, lying on the grass, tried to get a nap in. As time elapsed, the wait caused him to sleep restlessly, and he often woke to check for their return. At one point, he woke with a weight lying on his chest, one eye opening to find a slobbery face staring back at him. The sun's position was changing dramatically. He heard Siana call to Panda, whose weight left his chest, taking him to their site for feeding, while Shelby took Belle to Ella's site to feed her. By the time his sister returned, the men still weren't back.

10

CARL WASN'T SURE THAT what he proposed was a good idea. The only thing that spurred him on was Ella getting sick or injured. They had nothing for a child other than a partial bottle of simple fever relief. He sat in the driver's seat. Pete opened the door and then eased it closed.

"You'll have to help look out," Carl told him. "Any AI, anythin' floatin' that looks out of place—you tell me."

A grim nod from his passenger was the response. The weight of unspoken worry filled the air between them. They both knew there was a good chance they might not return.

After starting the truck as quietly as he could, he took a deep breath, put it in gear, and cautiously drove to the store. Pete's eyes and head constantly moved, searching the surrounding area, ducking to look around. Though Carl craved speed, he knew it would invite more notice than a slower pace. It wasn't far. Only a few minutes but, other than when Ella's mom had died in a car accident, they felt like they were the longest minutes of Carl's life.

Burned and crashed vehicles occasionally blocked the road, requiring Carl to drive on the shoulder or grass. The eeriness of being the only moving truck among what amounted to a vehicle graveyard was unsettling. Both men tensed at the slightest sound heard over the engine, constantly braced for the AI's attack. Carl noticed his hand shaking when he raised it to wipe his eyes.

Both let out of sigh of relief when they arrived. The lot held a couple of cars, the small white building stark against the shadowed forest backdrop. A decaying body kept the single glass door ajar. Carl turned the truck within the lot, backing as close to the door as possible, and switched off the ignition, leaving the keys in case they needed a quick escape.

"It looks like it's in one piece." Pete was hopeful as he looked out the passenger door window.

"Let's hope it's not already raided," Carl said, reaching for the door handle.

Both men exited the truck, left the doors open, and gagged as the smell overcame them.

"How do we move it?" Pete's words were slightly muffled. He had the neck of his T-shirt lifted to cover his mouth and nose. His eyes stared at the remains. His throat worked as he fought vomiting.

"Just step over it. I don't think we can move it without it comin' apart." Carl's hand covered the lower half of his face.

The sun had ravaged the corpse, and neither man could distinguish the gender. Animals and birds had removed a good amount of flesh, leaving exposed bone. Pete, spotting the stack of firewood for sale outside the building, grabbed one wrapped clump. He angled several split logs, propping the door open more, so they could walk around the remains. They reluctantly stepped in the bodily fluids, only to find that the heat of the past days had thankfully dried them up.

With slow, deliberate steps, both men entered, their senses on high alert, scanning for movement or sound. The absence of power was immediately clear: no hum of refrigerators or illuminated bulbs, just an unnerving quiet. Without the air conditioning and cooling of fridges, all the perishables had spoiled, the smell leaking through the refrigerators mingling with the stench of the corpse, causing both men to gag even more.

Pete pointed toward a door. "Look at that."

The steel door to the backroom was bulging outwards, the knob a melted mess.

"We're not gettin' through that." Carl noticed the door was fused to the frame. That meant the storeroom was off limits.

"What caused it?"

"I'd guess there's a computer in there or somethin'." His hand rubbed against a nearby wall. "Cinder block. It kept the fire contained. Explains why there's no electricity. The box is in there."

They both froze as a noise, a snap of a tree or something similar, echoed in the air.

"Let's hurry," Carl urged.

"Yeah."

Carl walked behind the counter, stopping, stomach tightening, when he saw remains lying there.

He forced himself to ignore it, despite knowing the owners, knowing it was one of his friends. Under the counter, he spotted a carton of paper shopping bags. He quickly put them on the counter. Bill and Patty used these so they could be burned in campfires instead of plastic bags filling landfills.

"Start filling these and put them in the bed and back seat as quickly as you can. Try to put the heavier ones on the bottom. We'll sort them later, but look for medical supplies first. Take all of them, even if you think they're useless."

Pete nodded, released his shirt, used only his mouth to breathe, grabbed a small stack of bags, and searched for first-aid items. If it looked useful, they took it. Carl, knowing he would eventually have to quit, took the cigarettes. Unfortunately, the selection was small, but he'd take what he could get. As far as he knew, he was the only smoker, so they were all his unless they needed to barter.

They avoided the coolers, knowing they'd risk food poisoning if they even attempted to eat any of it. They didn't touch the sodas, not wanting to risk it since many were in the same cooler as the rotting food. When they realized one cooler contained only water, they snatched those. Water would be a precious commodity when the AI cut off the supply.

Carl found the boxed pastry treats and grabbed them. He'd keep his promise to his daughter. Though unhealthy, the tempting sight of the numerous sodas stacked in a large, overflowing display on the floor proved too much to resist; they grabbed them all. Any junk food would be the last treat for who knows how long. They would also need the calories, especially given the amount of physical work ahead of them. They grabbed all the personal care items as well. A toothache is not something they wanted to deal with if they could help it.

Carl's truck bed was filled to the brim. They had to rearrange a few times, which was frustrating and took time they couldn't spare, but they didn't want to leave anything of value. Eventually, Pete had to sit on the passenger seat with several bags piled on top of him. They'd taken everything they could from the small building. As Carl climbed back into the driver's seat, carefully closing the door, he said a mental goodbye and sent up a quick prayer for his friends. In order to make sure nothing fell out of the bags stacked in the bed, he had to drive slowly and carefully.

***

Mary's eyes were full of unshed tears. Carol was sitting with her arm around the worried woman's shoulders when they heard the faint hum of an engine. Hopeful, the group stood watching for the truck. A flash of turquoise through the trees caused a sigh of relief to run through them. The men had made it back. They raced down the path to help them unload whatever they had found.

Jacob's jaw dropped as he realized how full the truck was. The men received an eager welcome, and Mary embraced Pete as soon as he was rescued from the pyramid of bags. Everyone grabbed what they could carry, bringing it over to the tent they had set up for supplies.

Ella, realizing her father had returned, ran to him and shouted, "Daddy!"

He swung her up into his arms, hugging her. Of course, the first thing on her mind after her father's return was the promised sweet. Carl searched the bags, chose a cupcake from a brightly decorated box, and handed it to her. A slim hand, trembling slightly, materialized before his eyes. A glance at its owner showed Shelby's begging face, blue eyes wide, strawberry blonde hair falling forward, framing it. With an amused smile, he gave her one as well.

"Thanks!" she gleefully said. The teen ran off with Ella to sit under a tree and enjoy the fruits of the men's labor.

It took a while, but the group sorted the fresh supplies, Carol writing what they had on a clipboard they had taken from the campground office. It would help them keep track and plan meals along with rationing out the personal items. Carl took Ella for a rest in their tent while everyone else reorganized their booty.

Shelby reappeared to help, almost shouting with joy over the tampons and pads she saw. Those with periods convened to discuss and categorize their preferred items, a quiet hum of conversation accompanying the gentle shuffle of things being sorted. After that, they decided to have a little party with dinner to celebrate the windfall. Ethan, naturally, didn't lift a finger. He briefly appeared, his voice sharp as he insisted on an entire case of soda, a request that was promptly denied. Lips tight, he stomped back to his site.

"Why is he here again?" Siana asked in a frustrated tone.

"Apparently to lord it over everyone else," Kathy retorted, annoyed.

"And in case we need a doctor." Carol sighed. "Unfortunately, we need him."

"And he knows it," Siana said.

The women pursed their lips, eyes narrowed at the back of the retreating man.

11

AT A COMMUNAL LUNCH, Shelby rushed in late, appearing shaken.

Scott sprang to his feet, eyes narrowed. "What's wrong?"

She just shook her head as she rushed to her mother. Carol, placing an arm around her, murmured a question as Scott strode over. The parents spoke in hushed tones with their daughter, and Jacob saw Scott stiffen.

Uh, oh.

The group struggled to hear Shelby's voice, but they heard her say, "He came into the campsite. He wouldn't let go," along with a small sob.

Kathy stood and asked, "Who, Shelby?"

Jacob raised an eyebrow. She looked as if she were going to take a pound of flesh out of someone.

The way she looks, I'm glad it's not me.

Carl spoke up. "Only one person isn't here."

The group looked around. The only one missing was Ethan.

A whistled song preceded him as he came down the path, hands in his pockets, looking like he hadn't just gotten handsy with an underage teen. Carl gave Siana a look. She scooped up Ella, promising her a special lunch at her campsite. She hurried past Ethan, carrying the child, who innocently waved at the man as she passed him, Belle following.

Scott, furious, turned and walked toward him. Carl and Pete jumped up to stop the raging father.

"How dare you touch my daughter! She's underage, you pervert!" Scott shouted, pointing an accusing finger at the surgeon, struggling against being held back.

"Really? Didn't you all say, not that long ago I might add, that she is now considered an adult?" Ethan tilted his head at them.

Kathy, her voice firm and angry, said, "For work, not sex, you pedo!" She stepped toward him as well, and Jacob had to stop her.

"Don't," he said. "Don't sink to his level. We'll figure it out."

"Yeah, Kaths," Ethan mocked. "We'll figure it out."

Kathy, taking Jacob by surprise, shoved past him and punched Ethan in the face, knocking him to the ground. Jacob saw Mary draw her lips in as her eyes widened with surprised approval.

"Kathy!" Jacob knew if they didn't get this under control now, the group could go rogue on each other.

Kathy looked at him with a stony stare. "I said my piece."

Carl, raising his voice to be heard over the clamor, said, "Look! Hey!"

Everyone turned to look at him, quieting down a bit.

"Look," he said, lowering his voice a little, "what Ethan did was wrong." As everyone nodded in agreement, he continued, turning toward the crying teen. "We have to do things right. First, Shelby, honey, are you okay?"

"Is *she* okay? There's a big difference between getting hit on and getting hit!" Ethan spat, rising from the ground while holding his face.

"Shut up."

All heads turned to Carol, who had both arms protectively around her daughter, speaking through gritted teeth. If looks could kill, her eyes would've slaughtered Ethan with a thousand paper cuts.

"You scared my daughter. You *touched* my daughter." She about hissed the last phrase. "You're lucky I don't cut something of yours off, plus break your hands. Think you could sew it back on, Mr. Arrogant Surgeon, with broken fingers?"

Ethan, lowering his hand, said, "Why are you all making a big deal out of this? You said she was an adult. I offered an adult activity. That's it. It's not my fault she overreacted."

It took Jacob, Carl, and Pete to hold Scott back, who was now cursing the doctor out along with Kathy, causing Panda to bark, adding to the cacophony of noise.

"Quiet!" Jacob had to raise his voice to be heard. The volume lowered, but the outraged anger was rising. He turned to Ethan and said, "You need to go back to your campsite while the rest of us discuss this."

Ethan opened his mouth to say something, but Carl interrupted him. "If you stay here, we will let them beat the hell out of you. We will put you in the back of the truck and take you to the nearest cliff where we will toss you off."

Everyone went silent. Jacob, not knowing what to say to that, knew Carl was serious. He'd kept his voice soft, but firm. No hesitation.

Ethan, pressing his lips together, seemed to realize it as well, turned and stomped back to his campsite.

Carl turned back to Shelby. "Tell us what happened. Just the facts, okay?"

She nodded, blowing her nose in a tissue someone had passed to her. "I had opened my tent flap, and he was standing there. Before I could stop him, he walked in. He didn't touch me, but he got so close I had to back up."

Jacob watched Scott's fists clench.

"He asked..." Her face reddened.

No one rushed her, letting her tell it in her own time.

Carol said, "It's okay, baby. No one is upset with you. Only love here."

Kathy, tone gentle, said, "That's right, sweetie. We just need to know, because we can't allow this within the group. We need to decide what to do with him. It's not your fault. None of this is your fault."

Tears slid down Shelby's face as she said, "It's embarrassing."

Carol told her, "Then whisper it to me. I'll say it."

Shelby shakily turned her head to her mom and murmured into her ear. The only change in Carol was a tightening of her jaw.

Her eyes looked at the group as she repeated, "He asked if she'd slept with any boyfriends. She said no. He offered to make her first time very good, then reached out to touch her face."

Kathy scoffed. "The man wanted a teenage virgin."

"Honey, being a virgin is nothing to be ashamed of. Personally, I'm glad to hear it." Scott's face looked proud of his daughter.

"Scott!" Carol chided, eyes wide.

"What? Aren't you glad to hear it?" His arms spread out from his sides as he looked at his wife.

"Seriously? Now?" Carol just stared at him.

"Sorry." Scott seemed to realize it was poor timing and looked down, arms falling back down, ashamed.

Despite the tears, a small smile twitched at the corners of Shelby's mouth at her parents' words. It seemed her father's poor timing was nothing new.

"Tell us the rest, Shelby." Carl kept his voice gentle.

She took a deep, shaky breath. "I refused and tried to walk past him. He grabbed my arm, tried to talk me into it, saying my parents didn't need to know, we could meet privately and wouldn't let me go. I kept telling him no. He wrapped his arm around me and kept trying to push himself against me. One of his hands was touching my butt." Her voice shook. "I finally kicked him, yanked away, and ran. I was so scared."

"Shelby, why don't you go to our campsite and sit with Siana, okay? We're going to talk about what to do to punish him," Jacob murmured to her.

Kathy interjected, "I'm gonna go with Carl's plan."

"Why can't I stay? I want to decide too." Her face was resolute.

Jacob nodded. "It's within your rights to do so."

Shelby sat down with her parents on either side, Carol keeping hold of her hand.

"Since my sister isn't here, we can discuss or take the evening to calm down, think, and meet back in the morning. I can bring her up-to-date, so she can vote as well."

"As much as I hate to say it, I think we should all take tonight to think. I'm sure we all want him out. The issue is how to keep him from coming back into camp." Pete's voice grew contemplative as he spoke.

Slow nods came from various people.

"Pete's right," Jacob said. "We haven't discussed much in terms of rules and punishments for this type of thing. There is no police to call, no judges. We're it. Vigilante-style justice is something we need to avoid. We need to go over what we can let go, what we need to punish, what we need to expel people for, and maybe more."

"You mean, like execute?" Mary asked, her voice tremulous.

Jacob turned to her. "I'll be honest. We are in a world without the rule of law. If someone wants to take one of our women, are we going to stand by and let them? What about our supplies? We need to decide what we will do with someone who tries to kill one of us. What would we do if Ethan had"—he turned to face her—"sorry Shelby—raped her?"

Scott, barely suppressing his anger, said, "I'd have killed him. None of you could've stopped me."

Jacob gave him a nod of acknowledgment, not pointing out they outnumbered him, though he wasn't sure anyone would stop him. In fact, he was pretty sure Kathy would've helped as well as Carl. "This is why we need to discuss and decide without the emotions of a recent event. What is worth the death penalty? A beating? Our options for punishment are severely limited." He sighed.

Faces, mirroring the sobering reality that had just hit all of them, looked at each other. Each one had to search their conscience and decide what he or she was willing to accept or do if someone broke their rules.

12

AFTER DINNER, UNDER THE setting sun, Carol noticed something odd during her watch. She hurried to Jacob and Carl, who were sitting around a crackling campfire, smoke filling the air, with Siana and Ella, the sweet smell of roasting marshmallows wafting from their sticks as they prepared s'mores. The store had a ton of ingredients, and each site received a portion.

"Hey, I saw someone leaving the supply tent. I couldn't tell who it was. The sun was in my eyes, but it looked like a man." Carol's tone was urgent.

Carl and Jacob looked at each other before rising. Glancing at Siana, who nodded, once again agreeing to stay with Ella before either could say anything. Ella trusted Siana, and they didn't want her to witness whatever they had to do. The other two, urged on by Carol's urgent description of what she saw, hastened toward the supply tent. When they arrived, Carl unzipped it, pulling the clipboard off the stacked cases of water to double-check amounts. His lips tightened as the amount on the paper and what was in front of them didn't match.

"Someone's stealing," he murmured, his tone angry.

A sigh escaped Jacob. Carol's hand flew to her mouth.

"I think we all may suspect the same person," Jacob said resigned. The others nodded grimly.

"Let's visit each site. Ask questions and search the tents. We'll leave him for last after we have the others with us," Carl said.

Carol said, "I think we know you guys didn't do it. You've been fair with the food and have no reason to hide any. You were also with each other and the little one."

Jacob nodded, his face betraying none of the relief he felt. As soon as the words left Carl's mouth, his stomach churned as he remembered he'd hidden food in his tent.

"Let's start with Pete. He's been pretty easygoing, so I doubt he did it, but he's most likely to let us search. Once he does, others will follow suit," Carl said.

Carol suggested, "Do ours and Shelby's first. That will help him allow it."

With the still-setting sun near the horizon, casting long shadows through the pines, everyone headed toward Carol's family's campsite. The automatic campground lights flickered on, their soft light guiding the way through the darker areas.

Shelby, being a teen, had her own tent for privacy. For safety, she stayed at the same site as her parents, though it hadn't helped her earlier. Carol, Scott, and Shelby stood by while Carl and Jacob investigated their tents plus the surrounding areas.

They finished, finding nothing. They all walked over to Mary and Pete's. Once the couple heard what had happened, they willingly allowed a search, which also turned up nothing.

Their group growing larger—everyone wanted to know who did it, though they all knew—they went to Kathy's site. Kathy was more than willing to allow a search, ticked off that someone would allow the rest to go hungry. With every step toward Ethan's, their anger intensified, the rhythmic thud of their feet keeping beat to the rising tide of resentment in the group.

The fire crackled merrily, casting flickering shadows on his face as he sat in his chair, water bottle in his lap, sunglasses perched on his nose—he looked as if he'd anticipated their arrival. Jacob hated those glasses and frequently stopped himself from taking them off his face.

"Ethan," Jacob said, "someone stole food from the supply tent. We're searching tents to see who it was, and we're here to search yours." He wasn't in the mood to be anything other than direct. In fact, he may help the others beat the crap out of the man.

Ethan remained sitting, his eyes fixed on them, the silence amplifying the intensity of the moment.

Jacob, resisting the urge to hit the arrogance and smugness off his face, started to speak, but Carl interrupted him.

Carl said, "I'm goin' to do it now."

He didn't wait for Ethan's permission. His strides were deliberate, carrying him directly into Ethan's tent, the fabric yielding slightly as he entered.

"Holy—! He's taken a lot!" Carl's deep voice, like thunder, boomed from inside. They had clearly not seen the previous thefts.

Scott stepped inside and let out a gasp at the sheer volume of what Ethan had hidden. "What the hell?"

Jacob, moving toward Ethan, said, "You're going to be kicked out of the group. You're no longer welcome. If you don't leave, we'll make you. We will do exactly what Carl suggested."

He sensed the others' simmering resentment toward Ethan's disruptive behavior, and their eagerness to expel him, although they hadn't voted on punishments yet. Though he wasn't sure how they would enforce it.

Ethan's face stared, seemingly daring them to do something. It pissed Jacob off. His hand, grabbing Ethan's bare arm, hesitated. Instead, he hesitantly reached up and removed the sunglasses from the man's face, his body blocking the view from the others. Ethan's lifeless eyes stared straight.

Jacob called after he got over the shock. "He's dead."

Stunned, no one spoke. Carl and Scott exited the tent, hurrying over to Jacob.

"What?" Carol's disbelieving voice broke the silence. "How?"

The Haven

The campground lights flickered and died, plunging the area into an inky blackness.

***

Concerned voices, filled with worry and fear, talked over each other. They had moved themselves to the main campfire ring after removing everything of value from Ethan's site, lighting any lanterns they had so they could see. The dead man's water bottle was checked; the level was only a quarter down. No one touched the mouthpiece or the water itself. They left him to the wildlife.

Jacob called for quiet, his voice a low rumble that cut through the noisy chatter.

"It looks like the water and electrical were done around the same time. Anyone who recently filled their water and drank it, tell us how long ago you did it."

Mary spoke up. "I filled mine this afternoon before dinner. I drank all of it. I'm not sick or nothing."

Kathy said, "I just refilled mine, but dumped them after I saw him dead. I used some of my already-filled water buckets to wash them out." She told them she had poured safe water into a portable tub and scrubbed them with dish soap and a bottle brush, rinsing with clean water.

Jacob nodded. "I think we should dump any water refilled after dinner. We used the water from the campground faucet to make dinner, so I know it wasn't poisoned then."

Carol, voice full of fear, said, "Our neighbor has been right. I don't want to stay here while being hunted."

Everyone nodded. With the agreed-upon time here, it was time to move. The weight of the decision settled on them.

"We planned everything. We knew this was coming. I believe Mary and Pete gathered any carts they found?" Jacob looked to the couple for confirmation. Both nodded.

Pete said, "We put them around the back of the supply tent. There were only four. We also found a kid's wagon. We thought Ella could ride in it."

Carl gave a curt nod of his head, his eyes conveying his gratitude.

"Plus mine is five. That's one for each site to pull. Each cart should have a varied supply: medicines, women's products, water, food. If we have to abandon one, the other carts should have enough to be okay. Basically, don't put all our eggs in one basket. Everyone made their go-bags already, correct?"

Heads nodded.

Carl said, "I suggest that on the day we leave, we have a big breakfast cookin' up all the perishables as early as possible. Any leftovers can be fed to the dogs. Get ourselves dressed, gather everythin', and get movin'. It's a long walk."

Unfortunately, after much discussion, they realized they couldn't use his truck. The engine alone would announce their presence to hunters and AI cops. It had been an enormous risk for him to have driven it earlier.

Jacob added, "If you're not used to walking long distances, put on two pairs of thin socks or a thick pair. The blisters are going to be bad. Make sure you're packing bandages. Let's head to bed, regroup in the morning, and work on getting our packs and carts loaded. Don't worry about the tents or anything."

The somber group, heads bowed, moved together in silence, their footsteps muffled on the camp paths. Until now, it had been an extended camping trip. The moment of truth arrived. The struggle for survival had begun.

13

AFTER BREAKFAST, THE AROMA of wood smoke still lingered in the air as they met at the canvas supply tent, its flaps fluttering in the breeze.

"We cannot take everything," Jacob stated.

"Can't we stay another day?" Shelby was eyeing the junk food wistfully, as was her mother.

"We are. We need to stock calories," Siana said. "We need to eat what we can without making ourselves sick. For packing, water is the utmost priority, followed by nutritious, calorie-dense foods. We're going to need the energy from calories to pull the carts and walk."

While Ella blew bubbles at the dogs, who were chasing and snapping at them, causing her to giggle, the adults began sorting. Water went into each cart first. Scott and Pete ran around the campground, trying to find anything with wheels that could hold food. They returned with a few more wheeled items. Jacob ran back to his campsite and grabbed the wheeled cooler he'd found the first day. They discussed how much each item could carry without breaking, as well as how much each person could pull.

The wheels on the cooler weren't strong, so they packed it with light items. Because Ella's wagon, used when she would be too tired to walk, would carry her, her little dog, her backpack, and a collapsible dog bowl, they packed only a few lighter items in it.

It took several hours and much discussion. Anything that could mold or spoil in the sun was set aside for that day's meals. They compared the canned food in terms of calories and nutritional value. To their dismay, they discovered that their group's resources were drastically insufficient for the distance they had to travel, especially when it had to fit in the carts. Even if they could take Carl's truck, the people displaced the space for food. Uneasiness about making the trip grew, and Mary questioned the wisdom.

"I can forage," Jacob said, hoping to allay fears. "We're getting into summer, so there should be berries and other items I can find to supplement our food. We should be able to find wild yams, onions, and garlic. We can fish the streams and set small traps for game." He didn't know what would happen, but the group's initial fear, growing as they sat there, wasn't a good start.

With their supplies finally sorted, carts and backpacks full, the group began preparing a banquet for the rest of the day. Ella, thrilled she could eat unlimited junk food—within reason—danced around, singing a made-up song about how happy she was, causing the rest of the group to smile.

After eating the last meal of the day, on their way to their spot, Siana swore to Jacob that if she saw one more neon-pink, artificially sweetened snack cake, she'd puke. He agreed. Even the chocolate ones had lost their appeal.

As they sat around the crackling campfire Jacob had started, the rhythmic chirping of cicadas filled the night air. Her brother noticed the slump of Siana's shoulders and the way her eyes were downcast, realizing she looked sad.

"What's up?" Jacob murmured.

Her gaze stayed fixed on the fire, the flames' reflection dancing on her face. "I was just thinking about Mel and the other nurses. Is it wrong to hope it was quick? That they didn't suffer? That the children and other patients... staff... didn't suffer?"

"No, it's not wrong." He thought of his own coworkers and wondered if any had survived.

"I keep thinking if you hadn't talked me into this trip, I would probably be dead." Her voice cracked.

A sobering silence fell between them as the gravity of the thought settled in.

"This is why, as your big brother, you should listen to me," he teased. Born first, he never let her forget it. He dodged the small stone she threw at him, though she couldn't hide her small smile.

"It's not my fault you pushed your way past me." She gave him a mock-accusing glare.

Their mom's last scan predicted Siana's arrival first, but Jacob surprised everyone by emerging first; both babies were large, a stark contrast to their mother's petite frame. Jacob had shocked the doctors, squeezing past his sister. They fell into their decades-old teasing argument over their births. If only for a second, their sibling banter made life seem a bit more normal for both of them.

***

The sunrise cast a warm glow as Scott roused everyone, with the sounds of birdsong filling the air. Unfortunately, he had the last watch, meaning he'd be losing precious sleep and facing a long, tiring day. Carl and Carol cooked up a big breakfast for the group to share. Much to the dogs' delight, they got the leftovers.

Carl had retrieved trail maps from the camp store. Thankfully, it had a cash box—which was unheard of nowadays—and no electronics. Everyone agreed that using the roads would be a death sentence. Before the trail ends, they should be at their destination. They would abandon carts as they emptied, consolidating supplies as they went. If they had trail issues, they'd condense what they could and try their best to get through the woods if necessary. Each family received a compass before setting out, with the general direction they needed to go along marked on a trail map. Scott circled the area he had seen on his neighbor's map on each. If separated, each could find their own way. One by one, they lined up with their packs on, carts behind them, and waited for the others. Finally, with one last backward glance, they began the months-long walk to Tennessee.

14

JACOB'S ARM WAS SORE, a burning sensation radiating from his elbow down to his fingertips. Even though everyone took turns between the heavier and lighter carts, the rocky parts of the trail made pulling them awkward. People took turns pulling Ella's wagon. Carl couldn't pull both her and a supply cart, so everyone had taken a shift. They left the dogs off leash to rest and catch up as they pleased. The seven-gallon water jugs in each cart, coupled with the cases of bottled water, added significant weight, making their journey slower, but they were absolutely necessary for their survival.

A portion of the jugs was already getting low. They decided to keep the jugs even after they had used all the contents. They could refill at creeks or rivers, then do what they could to sanitize the water. Even with the trip's stressful purpose, the stunning vistas, the scent of pine and the coming summer filled them with a deep appreciation for their homeland's beauty. Today, he was pretty sure they'd entered Vermont, though they may have already been in it. The days bled together, and he was losing track.

They'd started out hopeful, joking, laughing. Now, each of them felt an unfamiliar exhaustion, heavy and oppressive, weighing them down. Cramps hadn't taken long to start, as each person's body objected to what they weren't used to. Only those who, like Jacob, hiked regularly escaped the worst of it. The stops to ease the pain slowed them even more.

Kathy needed a bathroom break, so they called a halt. The women and Ella went off in one direction, the men in another. When a break was called, you went even if you didn't need to. That kept pee breaks to a minimum. To maximize daily distance, they strategized the schedule. Their destination remained months away—a chilling thought given their dwindling food and water, and the group felt the weight of this fear.

Gathering under the dappled shade of the trees, with the sounds of birds chirping filling the air, they sprayed each other with tick repellent and prepared their meal. They would walk a couple more hours until it grew darker, find a place to spend the night, and take turns keeping watch.

Thankfully, the trail had shelters, so they could stop to sleep in one. When it rained, they had to decide whether to stay or keep going. The days stretched on without bathing; a light shower wouldn't stop them, but a torrential downpour might, though they'd strip down to their underwear and wash. People held blankets or turned their backs to maintain privacy while changing. Rain was both a blessing and a curse. While it gave them breaks and a chance to refill water containers using a tarp to divert rainfall, it also kept them from advancing, causing them to use supplies without moving toward their goal. The trail also had toilets, and they took advantage of that. If the toilet was water-based, they didn't flush. They didn't want water usage to show up somewhere, giving away their position.

After she ate, Jacob watched his sister gingerly remove her hiking boots. She'd insisted on bringing personal and baby wipes to help clean wounds and genitals, especially after illness or periods. With the days becoming hotter, "monkey butt" was more likely as well. Siana winced as she cleaned her blistered, raw feet. The local store Carl had raided stocked blister bandages, and the group was applying them liberally. Because of the high infection risk, they applied antibiotic ointment, its slightly antiseptic smell lingering in the air.

Ella sat nearby, exhausted with the walking, picking flowers close to her. The dogs lay in the shade, panting. Jacob rose, leashed them, then took turns giving them a small amount of water in the collapsible dog bowl. Each dog eyed its bowl as Jacob took it away. He knew they were thirsty, but the water had to be rationed. Hopefully, they'd find a pond or creek soon, so the dogs could drink their fill. Their break finished, a quiet hush fell as they cleaned up, the scrape of plastic against plastic a subtle sound before Siana divided the leftover scraps from each disposable bowl for the waiting dogs. After they finished eating, she unhooked their leashes and let them walk free, leaving the paper products where they lay. Time would take care of it.

Relieved groans escaped as they finally reached the next trail hut. As they prepared to bed down for the night, they fell into their routine. Carl set up a sleeping area for Ella in the corner after clearing it of critters. Shelby usually slept next to her, with Carl on Ella's other side. Carol slept next to her daughter, with Scott sleeping between his family and any exposed areas. The other women would sleep at the feet of Ella and the rest, with Jacob sleeping anywhere he fit, usually at the edge of everyone. They'd discovered the hardest part about the open-air shelters was the spiders and bugs that would crawl on them in the night. It didn't take long for everyone other than the guard to fall asleep.

***

A noise woke him. His exhausted mind refused to function. He felt a hot breath as someone hissed his name. "Jacob!"

Jacob struggled to open his eyes, realizing it was Siana. His heart thudded as he met the intense gaze of black eyes in the moonlit darkness. The long, large, sharp teeth, warm and wet, nibbled at his hair, a chilling sensation against his scalp. He believed his heart had stopped.

Panda's low growl alerted him that the dog had awakened and noticed the creature nearby. Realizing the danger, Panda let out a series of sharp, staccato barks, the sound echoing off the shelter ceiling and startling everyone into wakefulness. With a furious yip, Belle's hackles rose as she stood on Ella, facing the approaching danger, her whole body tense and alert.

"Daddy!" Ella's cry of fear rang out. The heavy thud of boots hitting the floor sent vibrations through the wooden boards as Jacob heard Carl scramble to his feet.

"Close your eyes!" his sister's voice called out along with a metallic thunk.

He spun his face to the floor, causing the creature to rear slightly, and held his breath. A hoarse roar filled the shelter as a spray was released, grazing the back of Jacob's head, then reaching its target. Claws scrambled, scratching to gain purchase as it struggled to turn away from the pain and run. Jacob heard the spray cease as the creature spun, leaving the hut. The bear's pained cries receded as it ran into the forest. Jacob quickly flipped over before the spray ran into his face.

"Oh. My. Goodness." Kathy's shocked voice rose as she spoke.

"Are you okay?" His sister's frantic face looked down at him, the can of bear spray still in her hand.

"Yeah. Other than my pants."

"Your pants?" Her brow knitted in confusion.

"I think I pissed myself," he joked.

Sia shut her eyes for a moment, and he was pretty sure she was debating spraying him in the face next. "We need to rinse off your hair."

"Too late." Jacob's eyes watered uncontrollably, the intense, pepper-like fumes of the bear spray choking him and burning his nasal passages, causing him to cough uncontrollably.

It took some time and precious water as they rinsed his head. With each labored breath, the stinging spray lessened until he could finally breathe freely again. By then, the sun had started to rise. The group restarted after a quick breakfast of granola bars. They knew more exhaustion awaited them that evening, but they had to utilize the daylight.

Following their routine, they reviewed the carts to see what could be condensed. They were down to four now, the coolers having given up long ago. Though they rationed supplies, the first cart emptied faster than they liked. The walk was becoming mind-numbing. Wake up, walk, stop for a break, walk, break, walk, break, walk, sleep.

15

MARY WAS WALKING AHEAD. She had rounded a slight bend but came scurrying back, eyes wide.

Concern filled Pete's face. "What is it?"

"Bodies. Hanging from the trees." She gulped as she said it.

A shocked silence took over the group. Jacob and Carl set their cart handles down and moved around her.

"Daddy?" Ella's child's voice was curious. Shelby distracted her with the carved dog.

The men inched forward until they could see what Mary had seen.

Two bloated purple bodies, swaying in the wind, hung from thick pine branches that groaned under their weight. The stench of decay filled the air.

"There's a sign on one," Carl whispered. "Stay here."

"Carl—" Jacob hissed. *Obviously, the group would have to discuss not running into troubled areas.*

With a slow, deliberate movement, Carl edged closer to the bodies, his gaze sweeping the surroundings. Nervous energy hummed beneath the surface of the silent scene. A cold sweat broke out on Jacob's brow as he held his breath, watching and praying whoever was responsible wouldn't discover him. Upon reaching them, Carl scrutinized them before he rushed back, running past Jacob, motioning for him to follow. He did, and they jogged back to the others.

His breath coming in gasps from the exertion, Carl grabbed his water bottle to ease his throat. Jacob and the others fidgeted, their impatience growing with each passing moment.

With a sigh of exasperation, Carol finally asked, "Well?"

Carl swallowed another sip. "There's a sign on one. All it says is 'traitors.'"

Siana's eyebrows inched up as she stated, "Well, that's fairly ambiguous."

"What do we do?" Mary asked.

"We'll have to be careful. I didn't see anyone else around, but the smell was awful. I need someone to carry Ella and keep her face away while the rest of us get the carts through, one at a time. We'll need two people with weapons to stand guard in case we get attacked." Carl put his water bottle back in his pack.

Shelby volunteered to carry the little one, whose small hands reached up with a trusting smile as Shelby scooped her into her arms. Scott and Kathy offered to protect them while they passed the bodies. Both nodded at each other, their eyes gleaming with grim determination, and pulled out their scavenged knives. They decided Scott would stay with them while Kathy came back to help with the carts.

Carl, leaning over to his daughter, told her it was game time. Her face lit up with delight. "You have to hide your face in Shelby's shoulder." He wagged his finger and shook his head as he said, "You can't look up. You have to keep your eyes covered and on her shoulder. Do you think you can win that game?"

Ella beamed, nodding, as she said, "Yes!"

"Shelby will help. She'll keep her hand on your head as a reminder, okay?"

"Okay. We win Selby!" Her tiny fists pumped as a smile full of baby teeth showed on her face. Her mispronunciation of her name made Shelby smile.

Shelby carried Ella to just before the bend, with Scott and Kathy following close behind, knives held in front of them. Once Ella's face was hidden in Shelby's shoulder, Scott went first, the younger ones following, and Kathy brought up the rear.

While they waited, Siana prepared the bear spray, as they decided she would help protect the next group with the carts. They leashed both dogs. Mary took Belle along with Ella's wagon. Siana kept Panda's around her left hand, ready to drop it if need be. Both dogs were unusually quiet.

They can probably smell the bodies.

They focused on listening for any sign of an attack on the first group as they pulled their supplies to just before the curve. The fearful stillness of the survivors sharply contrasted with the quiet, peaceful sounds and activities of the forest. Jacob's muscles were so tense they were starting to hurt. Soon, they heard light footsteps becoming louder. Siana and Carl stood in front, weapons at the ready. Kathy soon appeared. Everyone exhaled, the sound of relief a quiet wave in the tense air.

"No one seemed to be around, but I kept watch on the way back anyhow," Kathy whispered.

"Did Ella..." Carl stared at her.

"She won the game. She made sure to make me promise to tell you." Kathy's eyes danced with amusement.

Carl, with a relieved smile, said, "I guess she gets her lollipop."

They'd made sure to bring a small bag for just such situations.

Pete and Carl took a cart each, with Siana and Kathy guarding. This time Kathy took the lead, with Siana bringing up the rear. Both men also had knives in their hands. Jacob stayed with Mary.

After another agonizing wait, Kathy, Siana, and Pete returned. Siana pulled a cart this time, as did Pete, with Mary pulling the wagon. Jacob and Kathy guarded.

As they drew near to the bodies, the smell became much stronger. Jacob had to breathe through his mouth to avoid puking. Mary refused to look at them, keeping the hand with the leash firmly over the lower half of her face, eyes straight ahead.

Jacob gave them a quick glance, their horrifying images forever seared into his mind.

What does "traitor" mean? What did they do?

He realized that groups may clash with each other as each would have its own rules to abide by. He prayed they would not run into the ones who had done this. Once they finally reached the others, they talked briefly about the bodies. Realizing there was literally nothing they could do, they continued their routine of walking, stopping for breaks, and sleeping either on the trail or in a shelter.

This repeated for several days until the trail went through a small town. Siana, still limping—she wasn't the only one—wanted to look for a pharmacy or store that would allow them to search for medical supplies. They'd run through the blister bandages and were quickly going through normal band-aids. Their supply of antibiotic ointment was almost entirely gone despite careful rationing. A quiet disagreement broke out. The others didn't want to risk it. In addition, the smell wafting from the town was atrocious.

Siana said, "I'll go by myself. Everyone else can stay here or keep going. I'll catch up."

Jacob refused, saying he'd go with her. "You're limping. You won't be able to run."

Carl said, "I'm not risking Ella."

Siana nodded in understanding. "I wouldn't expect you to. We can hide our cart here in the trees. You guys keep going or take a break."

Following a tense vote, the others decided to press on, Belle stayed by Ella's side. The trail through town offered little protection, and no one wanted to stand in the open. Scott crept through the open area, head on a swivel, the silence broken only by the sound of his boots on the asphalt. Once he reached the cover of trees on the other side, he motioned for the others. To avoid attracting attention, they proceeded one at a time, each person's muscles bunching, their senses heightened against a potential attack. The tense silence strained their nerves.

When the last one finally crossed over, Jacob waved, concern clouding his eyes as he watched their retreating forms. Siana was looking through the trees at the town. Jacob stored his cart out of sight between two nearby trees and leashed Panda, keeping a tight grip on the dog. He didn't need him running into places he shouldn't.

The siblings broke the cover of the trees hesitantly, their bodies tense, listening for any sounds of movement or danger in the stillness. As he and his twin walked cautiously through town, they quickly realized there wasn't much available. Charred timbers and twisted metal were all that remained of almost every building. The scene was a grim, silent monument to destruction. Siana's face fell, mirroring his own. Jacob, having given the leash to his sister to save her aching feet, ran ahead, leading the search. The shifting of rubble underfoot was the only sound. Still, their search was futile.

They walked as quickly as they could down various town roads, each step crunching on the remnants of a town forgotten, finding nothing but blackened buildings. The AI-enhanced vending machines lay as nothing more than misshapen heaps of melted metal and acrid-smelling plastic. There were no supplies here. A heavy sigh escaped Jacob's lips as they returned to the trail, and he fetched their cart, the disappointment weighing on him as they trudged to catch up with the others. The fallen town, a testament to their predicament, pressed down on them both.

"If every town is like that, how are we going to eat?" Siana asked fearfully.

"I don't know. We can continue to forage, but that's seasonal. If we can't find this supposed haven, we'll have to move south. If we're lucky, maybe we can find an abandoned homestead or farm still standing. The best bet would be an off-grid one." That would require a lot of luck or someone above smiling down on them.

They took their time walking because of Siana's feet. The dog wanted to run, but the siblings kept him leashed.

"I'm scared."

He nodded in agreement. "I am too. We'll take it one day at a time. It's all we can do."

They walked, both lost in their own fears about the future, hunger and exhaustion slowly taking their toll. Rounding the corner, they found the trail stretching straight ahead, bathed in dappled sunlight, trees lining each side. There was no sign of their group. They realized how far behind they were, but didn't run to catch up. They needed to watch their calories. Around the next curve, they saw them in the distance taking a break. As they walked to join them, Siana pointed at a cinderblock building, so small only a few people would fit in it, alongside the trail.

"I wonder what that's for."

Jacob, dragging the cart behind him, walked over to it. The metal door was unlocked. Opening it outwards partway, he peered in and immediately ran into a spider's web.

"Aw, man." He drew his head back, wiping the webbing off his face. Although spiders didn't bother him, he disliked sudden web attacks.

"It looks like a pit toilet of some kind, but obviously, no one has used it in a while."

She reached up and pulled a web strand from his beard. "If it's not too bad, I'll use it. It would be a pleasant change from squatting, and it'd be kinder on my feet." They hadn't seen an actual toilet in a while.

Sia found a long branch and used it to sweep the webs from inside the small building, sending their occupants scurrying. Screened grating lined the top of the walls, allowing light in while helping odors and heat to escape. Still, the musty smell from lack of use made it somewhat unpleasant. They took turns using the toilet. Siana waited outside with the dog while Jacob went in.

As he exited, they heard the faint sound of Belle barking. Jacob quickly pulled Panda back, silencing his excited whimpers, as Siana cautiously peeked around the corner, trying to get a glimpse of their group's activity. With squeals of delight, Ella and Belle were running around. Smiling, she informed

Jacob and took the dog's leash from him so he could pull   the   cart.

"That she can still run after walking so much is amazing." Siana smiled with amusement at the child's antics.

She barely heard Ella's high-pitched voice yelling, "Ball!"

With furrowed brows, Jacob and his twin stared at each other, a shared bewilderment in their eyes, before peeking around the corner again. They didn't have toys with them. Ella, standing in the trail's center, pointed upward, her gaze intense as she drew their attention to something above them.

16

THE GROUP STOOD STOCK-STILL, their faces reflecting the fear that clung to them like a shroud. Belle began growling and barking, advancing and retreating at the object. Her high-pitched bark rang through the trees. A shrill whine pierced the air, a searing flash of light momentarily illuminated the surroundings, and then Belle vanished, leaving only the stillness of an empty space. There were no explosions, no body, just an unsettling absence where she'd been moments before.

A sharp gasp escaped Siana as she took a step forward. The leash tightened in Jacob's hand, pulling her and Panda back behind the building as his other hand gripped her arm.

"Don't," he whispered. Facing the whimpering dog, who didn't like the noise, he whispered firmly, "Quiet."

As he quieted, Jacob was glad they'd taken the time to train the dogs as they grew. If they hadn't, he would've had to let Panda go, so he and his sister could survive. She wouldn't have forgiven him for that. He cautiously peered around the corner of the building again, his heart pounding in his chest.

The sound of Ella's desperate cries for Belle— a frantic, panicked sound—echoed down the trail, jolting Carl into immediate action. As he ran to grab his daughter, another high-pitched whine filled the air, a sound like nails on a chalkboard. Jacob saw Carl's hand reach out, there was a flash, and Ella was gone. A raw, desperate cry of anguish ripped from Carl's throat, causing Siana to wrench free of Jacob's grasp as she tried to sprint toward the gathering. In a swift move, Jacob lunged, his grip tight on her arm as he pulled her back.

With a creak, he opened the door to the dilapidated pit toilet, the cold air rushing out as he dragged his struggling sister and dog into the foul-smelling darkness.

"Jacob. We have to help them!" Desperation edged her tone, a raw plea barely contained.

"How?" he asked, keeping his voice low, but urgent. "With what?"

Siana's ragged breaths hitched as she looked around the musty, silent interior, searching for a solution. The sounds of their group's desperate yells, punctuated by the whining of the drone, filled the air; a chilling symphony of survival as they fought. Again, she tried to leave, but he blocked her path, his arm a firm barrier.

"I know you want to help. We can't do anything if we're dead. We need to wait and stay quiet so we don't attract it to us. When it leaves, we'll see if anyone hid. We'll look for survivors." His tone was understanding, but final.

She muffled her mouth with her hands, tears streaming down her face, her head shaking in desperate denial, the sound of her quiet weeping nearly inaudible. A sickening feeling of betrayal washed over Jacob; it felt like he was abandoning his friends. He had seen the drone flying above the child. It was out of reach. Without a firearm, they had no way to defend themselves. He wasn't sure a firearm could pierce the body anyway.

With each agonizing, slow second, a wave of dread consumed him. A desperate, terrified shriek sliced through the air, the sound carrying Jacob's name on a wave of panic. Mary. He squeezed his eyes shut against the call; the sound echoed in his ears. There was nothing he could do but listen. His sister huddled in a corner, her hands clamped over her ears, straining to block out the screams and whine signaling death.

Finally, a heavy silence descended, broken only by the occasional chirp of a cricket. Siana slowly stood. Their eyes met, a mixture of relief and uncertainty swirling within them as they wondered if it was truly over. Holding a finger to his lips, Jacob motioned for her to stay with his other hand. He turned, his heart pounding a frantic rhythm against his ribs, and slowly, carefully opened the door, handing her the leash.

Is it gone?

With a held breath, he peered outside, the smell of pine filling his nostrils as he scanned the towering trees and clear sky. He took a step quietly, constantly watching his surroundings. With a deep breath, he shifted his position, using one eye to check the trail while staying hidden behind the cinder block room.

When he didn't see any sign of the drone, he moved his head further out, so he could see better. Where the group had sat, their belongings lay scattered. With a last check, he emerged from behind the building, his senses on high alert as he approached the mess, the sight of destruction at odds with the serene scene of the forest. Part of him wanted to rush in case there were injured, but he knew rushing could get him killed. If he had to guess, he figured the sound of Belle and Ella playing drew in the drone. They'd have to watch their noise levels from now on. The dog concerned him. If no one was paying attention, Panda might bark, giving them away.

Upon reaching the area where his group had last been, he found almost nothing left of the people. Scorched backpacks, some missing sections, someone's foot, Carl's pack of cigarettes lay on a rock. He'd been trying to stretch them out, knowing he'd never get more. Jacob stood in stunned silence.

Scott, Carol, Carl, Ella, everyone—gone.

Claws on the trail caused him to turn back and look. With a slow, deliberate pace, Siana approached, the dog's paws padding softly on the ground, the cart's wheels rumbling gently behind. Her gaze darted around the path. He glanced over the group's belongings again.

Thankfully, there is no sign of Ella.

He knew his sister wouldn't like it if there were. The death of a child frequently caused her to come home and cry. He tried to talk her into a different area of the hospital, but she loved working with kids. He felt her presence as she stood beside him, examining the only reminders of their group's presence.

"How is there nothing left other than Kathy's foot?" she asked barely above a whisper.

"I don't know. It kind of reminds me of that sci-fi show. You know, the one that uses disruptors."

She nodded, knowing which one he was talking about.

He took the cart from her, moving it into the trees. His feet moved quickly. In short order, he had the remaining carts parked next to his. Realizing what he was doing, Siana began salvaging backpacks. She dropped each one near the carts, deeper into the woods, to hide them from the trail. Jacob agreed with this idea, and together they moved the carts further in as well. Their plan was to stay out of sight in case it returned. A small, high-pitched whimper, thin and reedy, reached their ears.

Creeping toward the sound's location, a small mound, violently shaking, revealed itself, crouching behind a boulder. Someone had hidden under a blocking blanket. The shape let out a quick, low squeal, vibrating slightly under Jacob's gentle touch, like a startled animal.

"It's us," he whispered.

The blanket peeled back, revealing Shelby's terrified face. Her eyes urgently searched around them, and finally her gaze returned to his. Jacob just shook his head at her. Tears overflowed. Her face crumpled as she understood her parents were gone. She wrapped her arms around herself, sobbing quietly in fear and grief.

Jacob's tone was sympathetic. "We have to gather the supplies. Stay here until you're ready to move. Stay quiet. We think the loud noise attracted it."

Shelby gave a slight nod, burying her face in her knees as she mourned her mom and dad. Siana walked back to the trail. With a tenderness that belied the task, she lifted the foot, then walked to the far side and buried it under a thick layer of brush. It was the best they could do for her. He watched as she turned, her breath catching in her throat, her eyes wide, her whole body stiffening. He stepped out of the forest shadows, worried, his head tracking her gaze. Mary's head, half-hidden beneath a bush, lay there, her lifeless eyes seeming to accuse them with a silent intensity. A low sob broke the stillness. Jacob, moving to his sister, blocked her view with his body, and steered her back to the carts.

"We should've helped them," she sobbed, attempting to keep quiet.

"I understand. I do, but we would have died along with Panda if we had. Shelby would've ended up alone." His voice had an urgency to make her understand. Though he saw it in her thoughtful gaze, the logic made sense, but the weight of this new life burdened her kind heart.

"We're going to need to watch how much noise we make. I'm certain it was the playing that attracted the drone."

"A child being a child. Killed for it." Tears ran down her face.

He wrapped his arms around her, not knowing what to say. Jacob held her close as silent tears streamed down her face, but he could only give her a few precious minutes before they had to leave.

"We need to get moving. It's possible the drone will come back looking for survivors."

He gave her arms a quick rub, then turned to the group's supplies. While she tried to get herself under control, he began reorganizing what supplies they had. To prepare for the possibility of abandoning the carts, they repacked their backpacks with essential items.

With three carts repacked, Siana urged Shelby to stand and replace her blanket in her pack. At first she resisted, but when informed the drones might come back, she obeyed. They left Ella's wagon in the middle of the trail for other survivors who may need it. With heavy hearts and a guilt-ridden backward glance, they each grabbed a cart, then restarted their journey, wondering what else they would find or lose.

17

JACOB SLOWLY SAT UP, holding his ribs from the kick that had woken him. His ribs weren't broken, but he would definitely have bruises. Jacob's face was grim, watching as the men held Shelby at knifepoint. He heard Siana's breath catch as she, too, woke and realized what was happening. Panda's low growl was the only sound. Jacob cursed. They had tied him to a tree with a rope to keep him from running off in search of food.

"Well, well. Look at what we found," one, whose body odor could knock out a moose, said.

"I'm sorry. I didn't hear them. I was thinking about Mom and Dad." Shelby's face held terror, her hands pulling on the arm around her throat.

Jacob held up a hand, motioning for her to stay quiet.

"I say we have some fun with the girls, then eat the man and the dog," a brawny one said. His voice showed no emotion. "We can hold on to the women, using them as we see fit, until we need to eat them too."

Jacob's mind scrambled. Out of the corner of his eye, he saw Siana's hand slide toward the knife on her hip. Panda was straining against the rope, his growl growing louder.

I need to stop tying him at night.

That he hadn't warned them concerned him. It meant the dog was running out of energy.

"Don't do it," the first man said. "I'll cut her throat, we'll enjoy you two, then we'll eat her."

Shelby's fear escaped in a whimper. Panda gave a sharp bark.

"Throw your weapons over here. Now," the second man ordered.

Jacob saw his sister's lips tighten in frustration before she removed her knife and threw it to them. He did the same, realizing she kept her pocketknife.

The second man moved to Siana, grabbed his sister's arms and bound them behind her back with vines. He did the same to Jacob, the vines biting into his wrists.

"You get to watch," he murmured in Jacob's ear.

"You two look alike." The first man stared at them. "Your sister?"

Jacob nodded, jaw tight.

How are we going to get out of this?

The man chuckled. "Hey, Finn, maybe we should have him do his own sister. Wouldn't that be funny?"

Finn yanked Siana's head back by her hair, causing her to cry out. "Maybe after I'm done with her," he said, his hand pulling her head to his crotch.

"I haven't felt a woman's mouth in a while." He released her. Siana looked at Jacob with scared eyes. "But I want that one first." He pointed at Shelby, who whimpered again. "I bet she hasn't had a real man, only some idiot teen boy who doesn't know what to do with a woman." He began undoing his pants.

Shelby's tears fell as she shook her head. "Please don't." Her voice was reedy, thin.

Finn smiled at her as he dragged her closer, the first man following. "Don't worry." His hand stroked her face as the first man laughed. "I'll make sure it hurts." His hand reached between her legs. "Has someone used the back door on you?"

Shelby cried out in fear as he gripped her.

"Leave her alone," Jacob said through gritted teeth. He knew it was useless, but he would not stand by silently.

Finn spun backhanding him.

"Jacob!" Siana cried out as he fell sideways.

Finn rushed to Siana, grabbed her hair, and dragged her to her brother, as Siana tried to keep her legs moving to prevent him from pulling off her scalp. "Want your sister? How about we bend her over that tree there?" He pointed at a large fallen tree. "And you can take her back end? Want that?"

Jacob glared at him as Finn shoved Siana's face to Jacob's. Jacob could see her terror. "Behave, or I'll make you rape your sister."

Finn yanked Siana back, dropping her hair. He strode over to Shelby, yanking her away from the first man. "Watch them."

The first man moved to Siana and held the knife to her throat while egging his partner on.

What do I do?

Helpless anger rose in him, knowing that if he tried to save Shelby, Siana would have her throat cut. What also concerned him was the fact that Finn showed no emotion whatsoever. He didn't even raise his voice.

Shelby cried out in pain as her back hit the ground, the man falling on top of her; her begging cries filled the air. "Please don't! Please!"

"Yell. I like it," he said, ripping her shirt open.

"No! Help me!" Shelby's hands tried to push him off of her as his hands undid her pants.

"Leave her alone!" Siana's yell echoed through the trees. "She's a child!"

Jacob tried to rise, unable to sit and watch this. His sister's cry of pain stopped him. A drop of blood traced down to her choker. The man's knife had cut her skin. Panda went crazy, barking.

"Sit down, or she dies. In fact, I can pull her choker off. Would you like to see her head explode?" The grin he gave Jacob was malicious. He turned to the dog. "Shut that mutt up, or I'll kill it."

"Panda, quiet," Jacob ordered. The dog whimpered, but stopped barking.

Jacob felt tears of outrage prick his eyes, knowing he couldn't save Shelby without sacrificing his sister. Shelby cried out again as Finn yanked her pants down. Her legs and hands struggled to get him away, flipping herself over to crawl with her pants around her ankles, caught on her boots. He wrapped an arm around her waist, bending over her. He ripped off her panties, causing a cry of pain, with Jacob and Siana both yelling at him to stop, tears streaming down Siana's face. Finn pulled himself out of his pants and pushed Shelby's legs apart as far as he could with his as she fought and begged.

Finn froze, released her, then stood, clutching at his throat, struggling to move with his pants around his thighs. It took Jacob a minute to process it as Shelby scrambled away, trying to cover herself with her torn clothing, and to pull up her jeans, gasping sobs escaping her. Everyone else stared at the arrow sticking out of Finn's throat as he choked and clawed at it.

"Finn?" The first man's voice was hesitant, as if he couldn't process what he was seeing.

He released Siana, taking a step toward his partner. Jacob rose and threw himself at the man, knocking him over. The knife fell from his hand, and Siana jumped to her feet, stepping on it. A strange noise caught everyone's attention, and an arrow embedded itself in Finn's chest. His eyes widened, staring at something to their left before his hands lowered and weakly tried to pull the arrow out, gasping for air.

Jacob turned and watched as a man with a bow stepped from the shadows, followed by a small group of people. One woman ran to Shelby's side, pulling out her blocking blanket from her pack to wrap the sobbing girl in. A man came up behind Jacob and Siana, cutting their bindings while another grabbed the man on the ground, who was rising to his feet. With one clean move, the man lifted his head, raised his own knife, and cut the first man's throat. He then pushed him back onto the ground, leaving him to bleed out, as the first man wrapped his hands around his own throat, trying in vain to stop the flow of blood. Jacob turned as he heard a thud and saw Finn's lifeless body on the dirt.

Jacob turned to their rescuer as Siana rushed to Shelby. The man, appearing nonchalant, extended a hand. "I'm Red. Heard the yells. We need to move into the woods before the drones come. That was way too much noise."

Jacob, speechless, nodded, grabbed their gear, and moved it into the trees away from the clearing. Siana and the other woman assisted Shelby, who was bawling, with a teen boy standing guard behind them. Once they had moved away from the clearing, and Jacob had fetched Panda, they stopped.

Red turned to Shelby. "You need to be quiet. I know you're upset, but unless you want to disappear forever, you need to stop. That was too much noise for the drones to ignore. Hopefully, they aren't in the area."

Shelby stared at him in confusion, breath hitching. She said nothing, just lowered her head and tried to control herself. Siana went through Shelby's pack and found her underwear and a shirt to wear. As the two women held the blanket, Shelby quaked as she dressed.

Red looked around them, then at their supplies. "What are your jobs?"

The sudden change in conversation, while ignoring what just happened, threw Jacob off. It took him a minute. "I'm a botanist. Siana is a nurse."

Red nodded. "Okay, you can join us, or we can take your supplies."

"You saved us only to rob us?" Outrage and disbelief edged Jacob's voice.

Red shrugged. "I'm not letting a teenage girl get raped. I'm offering you all a place. It's still survival of the fittest."

Faced with the possible imminent theft of their possessions, they joined the group, a decision born of fear and necessity. The fact that the leader was a skilled bow user helped. He also seemed to know what he was doing, as evidenced by his later hunting and shelter building techniques. Jacob was under no illusions. He knew the head guy wanted their jobs and supplies more than anything. He wouldn't hesitate to kill them if he had to.

Red—another redhead—had Jacob take point. He swiftly discovered that Jacob had a good ear for the noises drones made. Jacob had said nothing; he just grabbed his sister and hid under the blanket within the forest. The first time, Red had caught it out of the corner of his eye and hid as well. Others, seeing Red—who was walking in front—hide, followed suit.

Once, distracted by stolen glances and hushed conversations, more interested in each other than their surroundings, they'd lost Shelby and the teen boy that day. Again, Jacob intervened, silencing his sister's urgent warning; he could feel the tremor in her voice as she tried to alert them. No one was angry with Jacob for not speaking up. They'd all learned that noise only made it worse. Of course, Siana was upset that he'd stopped her. While he loved his sister and her caring attitude, he was losing patience with her. The death of their group shook her. It seemed like part of her refused to accept this new reality, and her behavior was going to get them both killed.

One time Jacob heard the drones, and he missed her arm as he went to hide. He'd had to run back to her, grabbing her and pulling her behind him. The drone came close to seeing them. After that, he tied a rope around their waists while walking, so she could feel when he went to hide. He walked ahead of her, so she had a visual on him. Others did likewise with their loved ones.

Another time, Jacob had barely heard the drones. He noticed it only because there were several. Three people moved too late. The only thing that kept Siana from running to them was the rope. Again, she wanted to warn them. A gasp escaped her lips, and Jacob instinctively covered her mouth with his hand. From his hiding place in the forest, with a quick glance from under the blanket, he saw they had redesigned themselves. They were sleeker, flattened, like airplane wings. The disruptors were also quieter and didn't make the strong white flash as before.

After the drones flew away, the group, now numbering five, gathered together.

Red asked, "Did anyone else notice their design changed?"

Jacob nodded. "I'm wondering what else they changed. I barely heard them in time, so they've improved themselves to be quieter."

Their leader nodded. "I agree. It's probably not the only thing they've improved. I think it's safe to assume they may start registering things we haven't thought of yet."

Red returned to the trail with caution, gathering up the deceased's belongings. Siana followed, taking any body parts she found and moving them to the underbrush. Red stopped her.

"Leave it. If the drones are improving, it's only a matter of time before they start double-checking. If they see bodies moved, they'll know there are more survivors. I'm not sure they'll do the same with the packs."

Sia, holding someone's hand, placed it back down on the trail. Jacob saw her tear-filled eyes as she returned. He felt for her, he really did, but he thought she needed to toughen up a little. If she let everything affect her, her mental health was going to bottom out. He didn't understand it. As a nurse, she managed to compartmentalize. He didn't understand why she wasn't doing it now.

Maybe she just feels helpless?

Later, when they were alone, he'd told her. "Don't set yourself on fire to keep others warm," he said. "You can't help anyone if you're dead. I know it's hard. I know it. You have to steel yourself against it."

She walked away, head down, without a word. His stomach churned with worry. This wasn't like her. She had a temper, yet he hadn't seen it since this started. Not that he wanted to. She was the stereotypical redhead in that regard. It just seemed like something inside her broke. It worried him. What also worried him was that Frank, one of their members, had run out of his medication. He did not specify the type, but his sister discovered it was psychiatric.

The group decided not to speak unless necessary to cut down on any noise that might alert the drones. Siana had learned a little sign language in school because of a deaf friend. She began teaching them what little she knew, so they could communicate without talking. Eventually, they began making up signs to represent what they wanted to impart as a group. Within a couple of weeks, they rarely needed to speak.

18

THEY WERE ABOUT HALFWAY through New York when the path shrank. A mudslide from the recent rains had demolished a portion, and the impact was evident. The sheer drop on the left with the sheer rise on the right made Jacob's stomach turn. It also didn't look very solid, as if it would give way any minute. The length, though brief, caused them problems.

"The path is still wet. This could be bad," Red whispered. "We'll have to be very careful crossing it. Too much weight on the edge will probably send the rest down. It'll be slippery. I don't want to jump it, I'm not sure we all could, and we'd lose the cart."

"I'd move the cart first once we're sure the path will hold," Jacob recommended.

Red nodded. "I'll check, go first, then you and Frank, Carlos, or Siana can lift the cart over."

"Jacob." Siana's whispered fear reminded him.

She's afraid of heights.

"Carlos or Frank would be the better option based on strength alone."

Carlos, who had been listening, nodded, then murmured, "With the weight of the cart, plus two people carrying it, it might be better for Siana to cross second."

Frank agreed, though he didn't look too thrilled at being last.

Red agreed and prepared to cross.

"Wait," Jacob murmured. Taking the rope, he handed the other end to Red, motioning to the path. Red, understanding, started to tie it around his waist until Siana waved her hand. She shook her head, pointing out another part of the path that was collapsing. They realized it wouldn't be long enough. A frustrated sigh escaped Red.

"It'll be too difficult and dangerous to untie it in the middle and keep my balance. I'll go without."

Jacob held his breath as Red carefully navigated the mud path, his feet barely fitting. He put his chest against the sheer wall as he edged himself along the thin remainder, moving cautiously, grabbing exposed tree roots where possible. Everyone froze as a small portion of rocky dirt under his feet fell. Red, looking back at them, made an almost humorous face of "whoops" before continuing. A collective sigh of relief escaped as he made it to the other side.

"Siana, go next. Don't look down. Face the wall of dirt or Red and move carefully," Jacob murmured in her ear.

Her expression showed her fear as she approached the edge. She was shaking, terrified. Hitching her backpack higher, she took the first step, then froze. Again he held his breath, bracing himself to jump for her should she slip. Not that he could do anything other than fall with her. Red, on the other side, held his arm out, ready to grab hold once she got close.

"Keep your eyes on me," Red whispered loudly to her. "It's only about ten or so feet. You can do this."

She nodded, but they could all see her breathing accelerate as she moved further down, using her left foot to feel her way over. Her breath came in gasps, and at one point, she stopped moving. No one said anything, giving her a minute to gather herself. Her body stiffened with what Jacob assumed was resolve, and she continued. When she crossed the halfway point, Jacob entrusted her to Red and turned to Carlos. They needed to figure out the best way to move the cart.

Frank would go next, being a man on the smaller side. He crossed over with care. Jacob, being the heavier of the two, would bring up the rear, holding on to the back of the cart. Carlos, holding the handle with his right hand, slowly began the walk. They had agreed to take their time. Carlos reached the halfway point when the cart tilted toward the drop as Jacob's hand shifted. Carlos looked back at him with wide eyes. Both froze. Seconds ticked an eternity as Jacob slowly inched his hand back into the middle of the cart. His fingers ached as he strained to hold it above the missing section of the path.

Once he was ready, he nodded to Carlos, and they started again. Jacob could see his sister on the other side, hands over her mouth, eyes wide with worry. He made a face at her, which caused Red to muffle a snort. Frank raised his eyebrows, eyes flitting back and forth between the twins.

Jacob's arm burned with the effort of holding the cart. When they finally reached the other side, both lowered the cart before collapsing onto the ground. Jacob stretched and moved his arm, hoping to ease some of the pain shooting through it.

Carlos stood, stretching his back and arm while signing a quick, "Ow."

Jacob nodded in agreement as his sister's hand came down on his shoulder. Her trembling told him how scared she had been for him. He laid his hand over hers, gave it a gentle pat, then leaned forward to push himself off the wet earth. The trail was thick with mud, clinging to the cart tires, requiring frequent stops for cleaning throughout the day.

Their supplies were dwindling fast, though Jacob was able to forage berries, wild onions, and garlic, dandelions, herbs, and yams, along with other plants, which helped a lot. Red hunted when and what he could. They kept up their vitamin C levels with pine needle tea only when they reached a water source and refilled. He was becoming more concerned as time passed.

We're moving too slow. At this rate, winter may arrive before we do. We'll starve.

The oppressive heat bore down on them today, a heavy blanket of humidity making each breath feel thick and heavy, and they knew they needed to drink more water. It made them nervous. It had been a while since they'd passed a water source. A stifling humidity clung between the dense trees, while the incessant buzzing of mosquitoes was a relentless, irritating chorus. With heavy steps and hearts, they trudged onward, the only sound being the scrape of their boots on the path combined with the underlying tension of possible drones overhead.

Frank giggled as they walked. His laughter intensified. A worried frown creased their faces as they stopped and turned, their eyes studying his features.

Red drifted toward him, arm outstretched, and whispered, "Hey, man, what's going on? You need to keep it down. The drones will come."

"We're all going to die!" A frantic yell ripped from the man's throat; his eyes, bloodshot and crazed, darted around wildly.

Jacob didn't wait. He pulled Siana into the dense undergrowth of the trees, the air thick with tension, and pulled the blanket from his pack. Her worried gaze, mirroring his own apprehension, reflected in her wide eyes as she pulled Panda along. Carlos immediately followed their lead and hid among the dense undergrowth. They pulled the blanket over their heads, leaving only Jacob's eyes visible as he watched and waited. Siana ordered Panda to stay quiet, though the dog didn't bark much anymore. He was thin as well, starving.

Red tried to calm the agitated man, but his raucous laughter and furious shouts only escalated, the sound filling the air like a storm.

"Come and get me!" He laughed, turning in a circle, arms wide.

"Dude, shut up," Red pleaded. "You're going to get us killed."

"Why?! We're already walking dead! Dead men!" He cackled. He stopped to glance at Red. "You know, she's the only woman. We could take turns." His hips gyrated. "Maybe her brother would help." He giggled. "One last hip mamba before death. I bet she'd feel really good."

Jacob and his sister stiffened at his words. A sickening feeling washed over Jacob as he pictured his sister's assault. His hand lowered to the knife attached to his belt. He would kill them first. Though he knew Red wouldn't agree to such a thing, he wasn't taking chances.

Frank shouted, "Come and get me!" already forgetting her. Looking up at the blue sky, the man reached up, his touch lingering on the cool, smooth metal of his choker before he pulled it free.

Realizing he would die if he stayed, Red fled into the woods and covered himself. Jacob pulled the blanket over his head.

It didn't take long. The tracker exploded with a sharp crack; the sound cut through the air, abruptly ending the laughter. They waited until they were sure a drone wasn't coming, then with a heavy sadness, rolled their blankets, carefully packed them, and walked away, unable to bring themselves to look at the dead body. Red salvaged what he could and put it into their cart. Carlos began pulling it. Jacob looked at Siana, but she kept her gaze down, head bent.

If she loses her mind, will I be able to walk away or do I die with her?

19

THE DAYS WERE STIFLING, draining them of energy. When they crossed areas of the trail that were asphalt, the heat rose into their feet through the soles of their shoes, which were being held together by vines Jacob found to tie around them. They usually switched to walking on the grass to avoid the heat. Jacob was concerned about their water supply. It decreased quickly, and they discovered no waterfalls or rivers as they had previously. It was incredibly frustrating. Despite the occasional trail bathroom with running water, they could not refill their water bottles because the water was poisoned, a torturous disappointment.

As they trudged toward the next town, a flash of movement caught Jacob's eye, making him freeze and retreat into the concealing shadows of the trees. With a concerned frown, Red inched forward, then abruptly retreated to the group, silently signaling Jacob with two raised fingers. Jacob nodded.

Siana signed, "What?"

Jacob stood, arms bent at his side like he was a cowboy in an old western, shooting at something. His sister just looked confused. Red tapped her shoulder, motioning her to follow him. Carlos followed both of them. Carefully, he parted a section of bush and signed for them to look. Jacob watched the fear blossom in Siana's eyes, their wide gaze fixed on him. Carlos looked little better.

The two crimson bots, arms raised, patrolled near their location, their metallic bodies gleaming under the sun, their presence a chilling reminder of the danger. Fear propelled the group as they backtracked down the trail. Once they felt they were far enough, they huddled together, their voices just above a whisper.

"Now what?" his sister asked.

"We need to get around them," Red stated. "The fastest way to Tennessee is this trail, especially since we can't use the roads."

After some discussion, they decided to try going through the woods until they were past the town. Removing their blankets, they wrapped them around themselves, using what they could to tie them around their heads and bodies. Red had paracord that they used liberally.

"What about the cart?" Carlos asked.

The container held the last of the dwindling water supply, its preciousness emphasized by the empty canteens awaiting refill, and what little was left of their food that they'd scavenged during their trek.

"Can we carry it? Or at least what's in it?" Siana asked.

They agreed they didn't want to lose the contents. After much back and forth plus experimenting, they figured out a way for the two of them to carry it and keep the blankets from falling off.

"I'm already hot." Red shook his blanket to cool himself. "We need to move as fast and quietly as possible before we overheat."

Everyone nodded their understanding. As they neared the town, following the well-worn trail, Red veered from it, heading into the dense woods, the air growing slightly cooler and damper. Carlos and Jacob picked up the cart and awkwardly followed with clumsy steps. Siana brought up the rear, keeping a watchful eye for any attacks. They hadn't gone far when Red crouched down. They had already agreed to watch out for each other, so they minimized exposing body parts to get each other's attention. Each kneeled down, following Red's gaze. The bots were near the trail.

That's not good. If they patrol it from the ground as well, we're screwed.

Jacob, behind a bush, watched them carefully through an opening he made in his blanket, trying to see anything he could without getting caught. His sister and Carlos had completely covered themselves, with Panda lying next to her. Red was also observing the bots.

One thing that stood out to Jacob was they rolled; they didn't walk. That would limit their mobility.

They may not be able to get on the trail. Maybe they're designed for paved roads only? Which begs the question: Do they have models made for off-road?

The group waited; time crawled, each minute a weight as they strained to remain still. A torrent of sweat ran down Jacob's face, each drop heavy and hot, obscuring his vision and making his skin prickle. He was glad they were in the forest's shade and not full sun. The airless heat of the blanket pressed down on him, yet he didn't dare move. The bots had come closer to the trail. He almost stopped breathing, afraid they'd hear him over the chorus of singing birds. A fly kept landing on the exposed part of his face. That was more torturous than the heat. With clothes clinging to him from sweat, and his body trembling near collapse, the bots finally disappeared down the road, their movements a slow, whirring sound.

When he felt it was safe, he cautiously removed the blanket, the dampness clinging to his skin helping cool without the blanket blocking the breeze, and grabbed for the water bottle in his pack, his body screaming for relief from the heat exhaustion that threatened to overwhelm him. He poked Siana, and she sat up, her tied-up hair plastered to her head. Panda had lain next to her, unmoving the entire time. It concerned Jacob. At this rate, they'd lose him. He briefly wondered about putting the dog down. It may be kinder to him. Red moved back to the group, also looking worse for wear.

"We need to get moving before they come back. We can take a break and cool down later."

Carlos, also drenched, shook his head. "I feel like I'm being boiled alive."

"Down some water and let's go." Red was firm.

Jacob knew he was right. If they didn't move now, they risked being trapped again. On the other hand, they risked heatstroke if they kept moving.

Siana, kneeling, drank some water from her thermos. Pulling a cloth from her pack, she wet it, wiped her face and neck, then laid the wet cloth around the back of her neck, around the choker. Grabbing his collapsible bowl, she gave Panda a drink as well. Once he finished, she grabbed her gear and began walking. The men followed her lead, wetting what they had available, feeling cooler afterward. Jacob again took point while Red and Carlos carried the cart. Once the trail rounded a corner, they rejoined it. Putting distance between themselves and the bots, they dove into the dense undergrowth and collapsed onto the soft earth to rest.

"Now they have ground support," Carlos said.

"They had it to begin with. Cop-bots, gas-bots, aide-bots..." Jacob whispered.

"Those looked like different bots. Almost like soldier-bots, but those are green, darker. This color makes little sense," Red said, glancing back in the town's direction.

Carlos asked, "Is it possible they're re-purposing other bots?"

The thought was sobering. If AI took all the bots from other jobs and put them on the road, travel would become even more difficult, if not impossible.

"If they add patrols to the trails, what will we do?" Siana's brow furrowed.

"We'll cross that bridge when we get to it, but we'll probably have to hike through the woods." Red's voice was matter-of-fact.

They fell quiet, each too hot to speak anymore. Once they had cooled down as much as possible, they stood and continued.

The day was scorching. After a couple of hours of hiking, the sun beating down on their necks, they rounded a bend and saw someone sitting on a boulder next to the trail, a quiet figure silhouetted against the trees. As they drew closer, the heavy-set man came into view, his chest heaving, sweat glistening on his brow. He waved to them; they waved back. His hand beckoned them.

Red, eyes narrowed, gave a curt nod to the others to proceed, then stalked toward the man, his body tense with unspoken wariness, pausing just short of contact. Jacob and the others continued walking, though he'd occasionally glance back to check on their leader. He could see the two whispering back and forth.

Curious for food, Panda approached the man, sniffing at him before padding silently after the siblings, the light snapping sound of Jacob's fingers echoing faintly. Jacob lost sight of them as they rounded a corner. Carlos waved his hand at them, and Jacob nodded. They'd wait here, out of sight yet nearby in case Red needed them. That someone was overweight in a time when people were starving was concerning. It implied something not so nice.

Within a couple of minutes, Red came walking around the corner, his face grim. With a questioning look, Jacob watched as the other man gave a subtle shake of his head. Red waved everyone to come near. As they formed a small circle, they touched heads. It was the best way to hear each other without making a lot of noise, especially the way sound traveled in the woods.

"He wants to join our group, but he offers nothing. No supplies, no weapons, no fighting or hunting ability, no useful job. He said his last group left him because he couldn't keep up." Red's whisper was barely audible.

"Do you believe him?" Jacob asked.

"That his last group left him because he couldn't keep up? No. That he stole from them? Yes. There is no way anyone should be on the larger side of life with the scarcity of food without taking it."

"There's no proof of that," Siana interjected.

"There's no proof to deny it either," Red shot back. "How much weight have we all lost since this started?"

"It's possible he weighed more and lost it," she retorted.

Red gave her a look of disbelief. "Our only decision is to let him join or not."

Their grim faces now matched Red's. This was an all-yes or all-no situation.

"So, he offers nothing? No benefit at all?" Siana's whisper was almost pleading.

"We've already decided this, remember? No benefit is an automatic no." Carlos's soft words reminded them of their agreed-upon group rules. "People who offer nothing will just waste supplies."

Jacob knew he was right. Their almost nonexistent supplies were insufficient for themselves, let alone an extra person who wasn't contributing. His sister's expression was one of quiet desperation; a faint tremor in her jaw, her breath hitching slightly, gave away the depth of her internal struggle. She dedicated her life to saving people, not condemning them.

She rapidly blinked back tears, hand shaking, and signed, "No."

Initially, Jacob believed she was refusing to abandon him; however, her pained, determined expression—her eyes tight with unshed tears, her jaw clenched—revealed her true intention: the man couldn't accompany them.

She may survive after all.

Though Jacob knew she'd hate herself for this just as much as he'd hate himself as he voted no as well. She was right that they didn't have proof he stole from groups, so he just went by their own group requirements. Red just nodded, turned, and continued their journey.   The others followed in silence, the unspoken grief of their decision hanging in the air. They were a somber procession. No one wanted to tell the stranger. In their cowardice, they left him waiting.

20

JACOB STRETCHED. A FEW weak rays of the morning sun struggled through the thick leaves. The air was already heavy with the promise of another sweltering day. He adjusted his pants; the fabric hung loosely around his thinner frame, the emptiness a testament to his weight loss. They were all in the same boat. He had found more vines, handing one to each, and they used them as belts to hold their pants up.

Time seemed to no longer have meaning other than day, night, seasons, and locations. He thought they were somewhere in Virginia, but he wasn't positive. Overgrowth already obscured many signs, and they only searched for those beginning with *T*. He could tell the days were long, but starting to grow shorter. Combined with the heat, he knew they had to be in late summer or early fall. It concerned him. They'd had little luck finding supplies. Fires or looters had destroyed or emptied most places they'd come across, plus each area had patrolling bots. If they didn't find this sanctuary before winter, they'd all die of starvation—if they didn't die of thirst first.

***

The group had found a river, setting up a small campsite to wash clothes like socks and underwear and replenish their water supply. They also gave each other some privacy while still guarding, so they could wash important areas. When they first arrived, Panda had about sucked down the entire river from thirst, thrown it back up, then drank again, before heading off into the trees to lie down. Thankfully, so far, AI didn't seem to bother the natural water sources. Exhausted, they all agreed to risk staying for a couple of days to rest and hydrate.

On their last day, a dead squirrel almost hit Jacob in the face. Reflexively catching it, he gave Red a look. Red's expression signaled him to pay attention to his surroundings. Over time, they'd learned to communicate better without speaking. The AI bots were getting better at hearing them. It had gotten to where any bodily sound had to be done with hushed caution. Out of a need for self-preservation, the guard nudged anyone whose heavy snoring could give away their location. Sudden sneezes would cause everyone to freeze and listen for drones.

Jacob set about skinning the dead animal. If Red gave it to him, it would go to the dog. The smell of skinned rabbit filled the air as Red worked on the two he'd hunted for the humans, his hands gutting each. He never hunted more than they needed. They'd each get half. Upon returning from relieving herself, Siana saw Jacob and immediately went to leash Panda. Her waving hand caught their attention. She looked around, leash in one hand, and put her palms up, waving them slightly.

The men, confused, looked around. Siana stared at Jacob, pointed again at the leash, then looked around the campsite. His eyes widened with understanding. Panda was missing. Jacob began lightly snapping his fingers to call the dog. He let out a slow, almost imperceptible whistle. Nothing. Searching their area showed no sign of him.

Siana stayed with Carlos in case the hound returned. The quiet search began, marked only by the occasional light snap of Jacob's fingers. Panda normally responded to it, but now there was no response. No bark. No whimper. No sound of paws breaking through the underbrush.

He wasn't sure how long they'd been searching for the lanky mutt, the afternoon sun beating down on them through the tree limbs, but he knew they'd soon have to call it quits. They couldn't afford to waste the energy they'd need for walking, plus night would fall soon. A bear could have attacked the dog. Hunger made him slower than normal, and he'd taken to walking up to anything that looked like food.

The minutes ticked away, each one bringing a subtle shift in the forest's atmosphere. He felt a rough poke on his shoulder, jarring him from his thoughts. Jacob looked at Red, who sniffed the air and gave Jacob a knowing look as he crept between the trees. He followed as the smell of wood smoke and cooking meat hit Jacob, causing a visceral reaction that made his stomach clench.

153

No!

Both men slowly followed the odor. Hidden behind the trees, they watched two men about seventy-five feet away preparing what remained of Panda over an open flame, his head on the ground nearby. Jacob felt a sharp, painful clenching in his gut, the acrid taste of bile burning the back of his throat. His dog. The desire to kill the men, to avenge his pup's death, swelled within him, a hot, angry tide threatening to consume him, his vision blurring with rage. A hand clamped down on his upper arm, its grip firm as Red shook his head, his eyes conveying disapproval, showing he knew what Jacob was thinking.

Jacob's mind replayed the day Siana had found the whimpering puppy, its fur matted and dirty, tossed into a dumpster by some heartless jerk. He'd jokingly called the pup Trash Panda, noting the dark circles around his eyes that resembled raccoon masks, and his scruffy, gray fur. The memory of the puppy, his tiny paws leaving muddy prints on Sia's new scrub pants as he shredded them with glee, her furious yell echoing through the house, and his head tilting in that cute, curious way. How fast he'd taken to his training. His love of people. Jacob's eyes burned as he tried to hold back tears.

We should've leashed him.

He knew it wouldn't have been fair to the dog, but now someone had taken the one they'd saved. Killed him for food. If they had securely tied him up, Panda might still be here. He could see a knife lying on a log near one man. If they had tempted Panda with something, it wouldn't have been difficult for them to kill him quietly. For that matter, the hound may have just walked up to them, wanting food. Instead, he'd become it.

His gaze turned and took in Red's bow. Red's look, a grim understanding in his eyes, coupled with his slow head shake, told him that while he understood, the fight over a dog killed by starving people wasn't worth the arrows, calories, or time. Jacob took a deep breath, tried to control himself, turned back to their camp, and slipped away, Red following. He didn't know how to tell his sister.

As expected, she didn't take it well. He just said the dog had been killed, so they left him. He was positive that revealing the complete truth would make it impossible to restrain her from finding those men— she would be unstoppable. The only thing that could set her off, other than children being harmed, was animals, especially someone harming hers.

She just stared at him, silent tears brimming in her green eyes and streaming down her face, leaving glistening tracks. Her breath hitched in ragged gasps. She gathered the dog's things—the leash and bowl—then sat by the river, the banks beneath her, and wept silently.

21

HUNGER GNAWED AT THEIR bellies, thirst clawed at their throats, and the heat pressed down like a heavy blanket. Despite their best efforts at foraging and rationing among the four of them, the cart was bare, and the remaining supplies in their packs were alarmingly scant. Water was hard to find, though all kept their ears open, listening for the sound of running creeks or rivers. Jacob was even having trouble finding good forage. Despite his best efforts, Red returned from his hunting trips empty-handed.

Jacob glanced at Siana. She was still sad about the dogs and those they lost. Truth be told, so was he. He had prayed nothing else would go wrong for a while. Thankfully, the days had been as peaceful as they could be, considering the circumstances.

A crispness in the morning air, a subtle shift in the breeze, hinted at summer's end. As the realization of their soon-to-be-lost forage sank in, Jacob felt a prickle of panic, the silence of the surrounding woods amplifying his anxiety. Fewer birds sang, and their melodies lacked the usual fullness, a sign of their impending migration south. Soon, the small group would look death more fully in the face.

The Haven

As they continued walking, a loud *snap* made them all freeze, the noise reverberating through the silent woods. The sound of a bow being drawn made everyone turn. There stood a man, his bow raised, his eyes fixed on them. Jacob felt his heart stop for a second. Another man revealed himself on their right, holding a sword, of all things. The four lifted their hands, palms open, a gesture of peace in the tense silence. Red's bow was on his back. As the only one with a decent ranged weapon, the men would kill him before he could get it unhooked. The second man, dark hair partially in his hazel eyes, nodded in a direction, obviously intending for them to move. Red took the lead, Jacob trailed behind his sister, Carlos brought up the rear with the men following.

Crap. If they take our stuff, we're as good as dead.

While they didn't have much, they did have filter straws that enabled them to filter river water. Jacob prayed these men were good, though force-marching them at sword point wasn't a hopeful sign. Concern for his sister flooded his thoughts. Realistically, they'd been lucky so far. Thankfully, she'd escaped any violent encounters other than Finn, and the vast majority of those they ran into were friendly and trustworthy. The group eventually broke into a clearing where several others were sitting or standing around a fire, with a large creek running behind them.

Three women, three men—including the two with weapons—and three children. As one, they turned and stared at the newcomers. An older, yet fit, man stood. His shrewd gray eyes took their measure before they'd fully entered the campsite. His short white hair seemed to stand on end as he walked toward them.

"Leader?" he whispered, close to them.

They all shook their heads. Despite the shared leadership during most times, a stubborn silence clung to the group. No one would betray Red, even in the face of questioning. The man stood back again, eyeing them, as he walked their line. In front of Carlos, he leaned forward and asked a question in a low voice. Carlos whispered. Jacob couldn't hear despite being the closest. The man nodded, then another escorted Carlos to a seat by the fire. The man stopped in front of Jacob.

Again, he leaned forward and whispered, "Job?"

Jacob answered in a low voice. "Botanist and herbalist."

The elder man nodded, and the second man tried to push Jacob to the fire. He resisted. Eyes narrowing, the man watched as Jacob's hand went behind Siana's back. The man's head tilted as he looked into her eyes.

Before he could ask, she whispered, "Pediatric nurse."

The man nodded, and this time, as the man escorted them to the fire, Jacob moved. Red soon joined them. The man motioned to a woman, who took the children into a tent. A little girl with blonde hair smiled at Jacob. He couldn't resist smiling back until she disappeared from view.

The man took his seat, picked up a piece of paper, and handed it to Siana, as she was the closest to him. With a subtle gesture, he indicated for her to read the document and then pass it down the row. When she finished, Jacob took it from her and read. The man's name was Mike. He was offering an invitation to join their group, share supplies, and look for the sanctuary. They had hidden supplies they would not reveal, quiet weapons, and their abilities were listed. The message at the bottom promised their release without harm if they declined to join. Jacob didn't believe that last part because of the look the man was giving him, but since Red seemed like he was more knowledgeable about this type of thing, he'd follow his lead—maybe. It was hard to get to know each other without being able to converse.

Red was the last to read. His head raised as he stared intently at Mike, examining him. The man withstood his stare, refusing to look away. Red, pointing at each member of his own group, motioned that they needed to talk. Mike gave a slight nod, and Red stood. He signaled to the others to follow.

Away from the fire, they huddled as Red whispered, "Thoughts?"

"I don't believe they'll let us go," Jacob replied quietly. "Whether because of our jobs or our limited supplies, I think he wants us to stay."

The others nodded their agreement.

"That means we have to agree to stay," Siana whispered.

Red stated as low as he could, "They have a lot of weapons lying around. We're outnumbered. They have hidden supplies, and the river is right there. I think Sia is right. Stay here. If it turns out the group isn't a good one, we can plan an out later."

Red turned and walked over to Mike, leaning forward to speak. They saw Mike nod.

Red returned, telling them they could keep their weapons, though no one knew if it was true. They froze, every muscle tense, as the sound of a branch snapping nearby sliced through the forest's quiet. Red, pulling his bow, caused their hosts to draw their weapons, the glint of steel flashing in the light, readying them for a fight, until they realized Red had aimed into the woods. Letting his arrow fly, a low grunting moan responded. Siana, having followed Red's gaze, was softly bouncing, her hands silently clapping. Red disappeared into the woods as their hosts watched in perplexed silence. Carlos followed Red, and Jacob realized Red brought down a buck. He rushed to help bring it in for dressing.

As the men presented Red's kill, their hosts' faces lit up. A couple carefully unfurled a crisp, clean tarp, laying it gently near the newcomers, and then began expertly preparing the meat, their movements practiced and efficient. Someone stoked the campfire and readied the cooking utensils. Both groups would eat well tonight. Later, they discovered their kidnappers had built a temporary smoker and had a large amount of salt so they could dry the game. Jacob couldn't help but wonder where the heck they got it and how long they had been here.

There's gotta be a homestead, farm, or something nearby that we didn't see.

Never shy, Red asked about the source of their abundant salt. Mike simply smiled, which made Jacob uneasy.

22

OVER THE NEXT TWO days, the groups attempted to merge, though Jacob's group resisted the unification. Carlos, on the other hand, had taken a shine to one of their women, Jill. By the third day, both would walk into the woods together. Red tried to warn Carlos, his friend, about the woman, explaining that her charm could be a dangerous honey trap. Carlos, unsure himself, backed off a little, but didn't stop seeing her.

Unlike Jacob's group's consensus-based model, Mike's leadership style at the camp was autocratic, with his every whim becoming a command. Siana was told to help dry the meat and, of course, she voluntarily helped with the children. Red's only mission was to hunt, so they could stock up on dried meats for the journey. Carlos did whatever heavy labor Mike deemed necessary. By the fourth day, Red's group was highly annoyed by their treatment. They received the same food and treatment as the others, but Mike's arrogant attitude angered them.

Siana once signed to Jacob, "He acts like he's a king."

Red gave a quick nod, having read her hands. The three were talking, in bits and pieces, about trying to sneak away, but Mike held all the meat they'd just processed. He'd also taken the meager supplies they had in their packs, saying they shared everything. It had effectively trapped them within Mike's group. He kept his word, and they were allowed to retain their weapons. If his group had been more like theirs, it wouldn't have bothered them as much.

Once, Red passed Jacob, whispering, "We're in one place for too long."

Jacob gave a barely perceptible nod. He agreed. It was just a matter of time before they were found. The problem was, none of them knew what to do about it. Mike might allow their departure, but under no circumstances would he let them pilfer any of his precious supplies. They needed their water straws and blankets at minimum; Mike had permitted them to keep the blankets but took the straws. Each of his group held weapons better than what Jacob's group held. They were feeling increasingly trapped, even though Mike had done nothing to physically hold them here.

Jacob and Roger, one of Mike's men, had gone out to forage, trying to find what they could to supplement their limited supplies. After working in silence for a while, looking through some of the dense underbrush, Jacob wanted more information about the group.

Moving closer to Roger, Jacob whispered, "How did you meet Mike?"

Roger, searching under some brush, whispered back, "Believe it or not, he's my boss."

Jacob's eyes widened in surprise.

Roger continued, "Jill was his secretary. Amy, her friend, was a worker in the welding shop. The other family is his cousin's. Ed and I had multiple jobs like welding, pipefitting, ya know." Roger sat back on his heels, looking earnestly at Jacob. "He's not as hard as he seems. His wife and kids were killed. Mike refused the tracker. He relied on other means to run his shop. He had rushed home when things started going south and found their bodies." Roger shook his head, eyes sad. "I can't even imagine finding your own kids like that. It did something to him. He kept a tight shop to begin with, but after that..."

Jacob pushed the mental picture of Mike's family out of his head, knowing it was probably how his mom had died.

"Why does he act like he runs the place?" Jacob was looking for insights into their "captor."

"Because he does." Roger shrugged as he leaned forward to dig up the wild onions they'd found. "We all agreed to abide by his rules in exchange for surviving together. The supplies he has hidden are his, as is this property. He owns it all. His house"—he motioned in the direction—"is about a three-day walk from here. He's sharing with us. Until he knows you, he'll keep you at arm's length. He won't risk us for you."

Thinking of his own group, that was something Jacob understood. His group before theirs. Then again, he won't risk his sister for anyone in either group. The men fell silent as they continued to search for food. When he was able, he shared what he had learned with Red and the others.

***

Jill was missing. She'd gone off into the woods and hadn't returned. Following a hushed, urgent conversation with her friend, Mike assigned search parties, their faces grim. Jacob and Roger were told to search west. Mike assigned the other groups to other directions. Unfortunately, they didn't have enough people to go in every single direction. The children were instructed to stay within the camp. Mike told them bad men were around.

"Once the sun goes below the tops of the trees, come back. If she's not found, we're not wasting time looking for her beyond that." Mike's voice was no-nonsense.

Jacob saw the muscles in Carlos's neck tighten like a coiled spring, and anticipated an outburst, but Carlos remained ominously quiet. Each group raced off, their footsteps disturbing the earth as they anxiously searched for Jill. After several hours, the search teams headed back, the silence of the forest broken only by the crunch of their boots on the forest floor, and discovered Red had found a trail of disturbed foliage leading deeper into the woods.

"Someone took her," Red whispered. "I can follow it, but with dark falling, it'll need to wait until morning."

"Okay, no one goes off by themselves tonight, not even to piss," Mike whispered.

Each of them nodded in agreement. Mike also increased the rotating guard. No one wanted the group's supplies taken as well. When Siana needed to use the bathroom, despite her frustrated protests, Jacob insisted on accompanying her, knowing his presence was both comforting and irritating. He could hear her removing her clothes.

"What are you doing?" he whispered, confused.

"I always get pee on them. It's easier to just take off my pants."

He heard her relieve herself as his mind tried to comprehend her logic.

"If someone comes up, you'll have to run half-naked. If they want to rape you, you've made it easier for them. Why don't you take the spade and dig a hole?"

"I lost it, which is why I started doing this. Plus, I'd still have to pull up my pants in order to run. That delays my getting away," she whispered matter-of-factly.

He couldn't argue with that. Soon, he heard leaves being pulled, then her dressing herself. She poked him in the side, indicating she was finished. He turned to take care of himself while she waited, her hunting knife in her hand. He was startled when he saw her holding it, as he hadn't noticed before. Once he finished, they headed back to camp. They needed a good night's sleep before hunting Jill down.

Red, leading Jacob, Roger, and Carlos, followed Jill's trail through the dewy morning grass, the sounds of birdsong filling the air. Ed, one of his other men, stayed behind with Mike to guard the camp. Each member of the search team carried their own pack of supplies, including their blankets. Mike had overseen the packing himself.

"Be back by dark," is all Mike said.

The chilly morning air made their breath visible, lingering as they searched. Without any food or water, Red didn't believe the kidnappers had gone far. Given they'd never heard her scream or yell, they didn't know what to expect.

Did they kill and eat her? Did they do something else? Both?

Jacob couldn't help the thoughts that clouded his mind. As the weeks passed, people became more desperate. It wasn't inconceivable that, driven to desperation, people might turn to the unthinkable act of eating one another. He briefly thought about times in history when such a thing had occurred. The Donner Party and Flight 571 came to mind.

After they'd stopped to eat some dried meat, and discuss options, they tried going further. With the long day stretching before them, they disregarded Mike's order to return by nightfall. They would search until they couldn't anymore. Jacob spotted a tree laden with near-ripe nuts and began pulling them from the branches. The others gratefully cracked the nuts with whatever they had, as quietly as possible, each chewing the much-needed sustenance.

After their break, they renewed their search. As Red followed the trail, the day crawled by, marked only by the shifting shadows and the growing weariness in their legs. Jacob and the others breathed raggedly from exertion. They had to stop soon, or they may not make it back. Just as they were about to give up, something caught Red's eye. Silently, he waved his hand at them. When he had their attention, he pointed. All eyes followed his hand and saw something on the ground within a small clearing. A fire pit of ash lay cold next to it. Slowly, they advanced, staying alert to any sounds or signs of others, weapons drawn.

The smell of something sweet and decaying assaulted them as they carefully approached, making them reflexively cover their noses. Flies surrounded the animal remains someone discarded next to a pit. Another mound lay on the other side. Carlos, drawing closer, hurried to the side and lost what little lunch he had. Jacob had to fight to keep his down. Red and Roger kneeled beside the broken form, their expressions unreadable, like carved stone. A grim silence filled the air. It was Jill. Her naked body was covered in blood and bowel contents, creating a gruesome sight. Roger pointed at her chest. Focusing intently, they observed the almost invisible rise and fall, a delicate pulse of life. She was alive.

How?

Jacob was incredulous. Her appearance betrayed a brutal assault. She was left exposed, her wounds oozing with fluids that he couldn't bring himself to investigate. Her jaw hung at an unnatural angle, a gag of rough cloth stuffed in her mouth. He wasn't sure she would survive. Carlos, returning, opened his blocking blanket, and laid it on the ground next to her, his face grim. After he pulled the cloth from her mouth, his hands grasped under her shoulders as the others watched in surprise.

Roger whispered, "It might be better to let her die. We don't have the supplies or medicines to help her."

Carlos shot him a glare, then continued moving her. A heavy sigh escaped Roger as, despite his words, he walked over to help. Once she was on the blanket, Jacob and Carlos hefted each end and began carrying her back. They were glad she was unconscious; the pain would have been excruciating, and her screams would have echoed through the quiet space. The ride wasn't smooth. Red and Roger searched the area for clues or any forgotten items.

The two men returned drained from the lengthy journey. Each rest break had offered only temporary respite from the relentless strain. The sounds of their own weary breathing filled the quiet air. As they stumbled into the camp, Jacob's gaze sought his sister, and she rushed over. His eyes met hers, and the silent scream in her wide eyes, a barely contained gasp of horror, revealed that she had seen their gruesome cargo. With a grim set to his lips, Mike approached Jill, then abruptly instructed the children and their mother to the tent, before striding into the dense, silent forest. Amy, Jill's friend, ran to the creek, splashing through the shallows to gather water, while Ed assisted the men as they lowered the injured woman beneath the dappled shade of the trees.

23

ED'S WHISPERED, "HOLY..." fell silent as her state rendered him speechless.

Siana and Amy worked on Jill, washing her so they could see the damage, whispering to each other. Amy gagged intermittently. As Red and Roger reappeared, Jacob heard a faint *pop* and barely audible whimper coming from the unconscious woman; the air hung heavy with the metallic scent of blood and feces. Soon after, Mike appeared carrying a small tote. He walked over to the women and set it on the ground, whispering to Siana. Jacob saw her nod and open the container.

Medical supplies.

Jacob made a mental note of the direction Mike had traveled. He wasn't sure how long he'd been gone, but it hadn't been long. That meant he kept supplies nearby. The men watched the women work while also standing guard. Though Red whispered he thought the small gang—there were signs of more than three—had left the area, they had to be safe.

Siana waved her hand, her fingers splayed as she urgently signaled for the men to lift Jill's legs, supporting them at an angle. Carlos rushed forward to help. Ed moved forward as well. Siana showed the men how she wanted them to hold the limbs. Once done, his sister's sharp intake of breath, a gasp that cut through the silence, told him it was bad. A somber silence hung in the air as Siana motioned, her eyes heavy with sorrow, for the men to return Jill's legs to the ground. Jacob saw her slump back onto her heels, the weight of the world pressing down on her shoulders and bowed head. Slowly, she stood and motioned for everyone to come close.

"I managed to pop her jaw back into place, but I can't fix her. I don't know what they used, but someone completely tore her perineum." Upon seeing a few confused looks, she clarified. "The area between her anus and vagina. I can try sewing it, but it's beyond my skill. She needs a hospital, a surgeon. Without one, with what's happening, she's dead. She'll definitely be in agony should she wake up. Without proper equipment and antibiotics, she'll probably get an infection because of the amount of fecal matter and embedded dirt alone. Something tore her bowels apart. She needs care and expertise we don't have."

"So, you're saying she's going to suffer greatly, enduring unimaginable pain and hardship, and will die anyway, while possibly giving away our location?" Mike asked.

Siana, after giving it a moment of thought, hesitantly nodded, eyes warily watching him.

Mike's face hardened, and he walked over to Jill's small tent. He crouched, reached in, and withdrew his hand, holding a pillow. He came back to the group and whispered, "We have a choice: either let her suffer or end her pain now while she's unconscious. She won't feel anything."

The Haven

"No," Siana whispered, her eyes widening in disbelief, a gasp catching in her throat. Amy and Carlos also objected, their faces pale and etched with disbelief, their mouths agape in shock.

Mike's face was impassive. "You just said there is no way to repair her, and she is going to suffer before dying. In her suffering, she will most likely begin crying out in pain. Correct?"

The conflicted expressions on their faces—a subtle tightening of lips, a furrowing of brows—confirmed Jacob's own inner turmoil. Do they attempt to save her, knowing she'd most likely die anyhow with great suffering, and risk giving themselves away? Or do they put her out of her misery, which would save them from discovery, but also make them murderers? Each looked at the other, a silent question passing between them about their next move, the air tense with unspoken anxiety. Mike stood silent as he waited for their decision, the tension thick enough to cut with a knife. He showed with the pillow in his hands that he'd already decided.

"Who?" Jacob asked.

With a detached expression, Mike pointed his finger at his own chest, devoid of any visible emotion.

"You can't be serious?" Siana's eyes, wet with unshed tears, beseeched Jacob. Amy's look joined hers.

Jacob hated this. "Sia, you're a nurse. You understand the physical aspects. Is there any hope?"

He saw the silent despair in her eyes, the slight tremble of her head as she shook it. "We lack the

173

necessary surgical skills, advanced medications, and sophisticated equipment. The damage to her body is too extensive. Even if she lived, her body wouldn't function correctly." She reluctantly shared the information.

Red, his eyes fixed on Jill, gave a slight nod to Mike before walking over to the crackling fire to sit.

Amy could only manage a desperate whisper of, "No." Her voice trembled as tears streamed down her face, her hands rising to cover her tear-stained cheeks.

Roger whispered, the words catching in his throat, "She's dead either way. She's our friend. Do you want her to suffer?"

With a slow shake of her head, Amy's unfocused gaze remained on him, her hair swayed in the breeze. Jacob understood her despair. With Jill's life hanging in the balance, she—like they—grappled with the horrific decision of ending her friend's suffering or letting her die a slow, torturous death. If it had been his sister, Jacob wasn't sure what he'd do.

That's not true. I wouldn't let her suffer even if I had to do it myself. Though, I would most likely hunt down the men who did it.

With her hands pressed to her mouth to deaden the sound of her weeping, Amy retreated to the fire pit, her back to Jill, hiding her distress. Roger, giving Mike a nod, followed her. Overwhelmed with emotion, Carlos nodded, tears falling down his face, joining the others in their silent grief. They all could see he had developed feelings for her, and this decision weighed heavily on him. Jacob, putting a comforting arm around his sister, almost pulled her away, but her heels dug into the dusty ground, refusing to budge. He saw the desperation in her eyes, the way her shoulders tightened as she fought with this agonizing decision.

"Let her go," he whispered.

"No, the human body can do amazing things. She could heal, could live." Her whisper was desperate, and even to him, it sounded like she was trying to convince herself.

"Sia, I know you want to save her, but we have to be realistic. If she lives, it will be weeks of healing before she can move—if she can move. What are the odds she'll heal without extreme or permanent pain? Without permanent damage? What are the odds of her not getting infected? Will she be able to walk? Run? Will she be angry with us for not letting her go?"

He watched her jaw quiver as tears slid down her cheeks. Though still against it, she allowed him to pull her away. Jacob knew his twin and knew she understood the logistics. Her compassion and empathy made it difficult for her. A wave of self-loathing would wash over her, extending to them as well; yet, he was certain she knew, deep down, it was the best option.

No one watched as Mike smothered Jill with her own pillow. It was anticlimactic. There was no fighting, no sound, no fanfare. Just the soft shifting of the fabric as Mike brought it down on her face. Within minutes, it was done.

Mike asked Siana, their resident medical expert, to double-check. As she stood and moved toward the woman, Jacob saw her hands tremble, her breath hitching in her chest. They all watched as Sia "officially" declared her dead, tears still streaming down her face. Carlos stood, walked over to Jill, and carefully wrapped her body in his blanket, now soaked with her blood. He struggled to lift her, and Ed rushed over to help him. Together, they carried her into the woods. When they returned, Carlos took Jill's blanket for himself, leaving her wrapped in his.

Mike whispered, "Are the men gone, or are they still in the area?" The set of his jaw made Jacob think Mike planned to hunt them down.

Before they could come to terms with what had happened, or answer the question, Jacob heard the almost silent whine. Because Siana wasn't tied to him, he had to lunge for her. He grabbed her arm and pulled her toward the trees. He saw a boulder and scrambled behind it, unrolling their blanket.

Siana whispered, "The children," as she helped him cover themselves.

Red, knowing what Jacob's sudden move meant, grabbed his blanket, whispered, "Hide!" into the tent with the kids, and bolted into the woods.

The others, following their lead, did the same. Ed landed near Jacob and his sister. Jacob could see him staring at him from under his blocking blanket, terror-filled eyes wide within the shadowed space, breath heaving rapidly and quietly. Jacob cloaked himself, and the other man disappeared from view.

The whine grew louder, and soon it was clear there were several drones. Jacob held his breath, trying to slow his breathing, so he wouldn't make any noise. Straining to listen, he thankfully heard nothing from his sister. He didn't dare look at her or move.

A child's panic-filled scream made him freeze. It abruptly cut off.

Jacob felt his sister move and grabbed her arm, whispering, "No!" as quietly as he could.

Another child, crying in fear, covered his voice before the child was silenced. Their mother, screaming and cursing the drones, was next. Low sobbing and a frightened voice called, "Mama," before it, too, fell silent.

Jacob's heart leaped into his throat, and a cold sweat broke out on his skin as the blanket slipped, revealing one of his eyes.

Do I move it? Do I not move?

He wasn't sure what the right decision was and prayed the boulder kept them hidden. Ed, in a more open area, was still, but Jacob could see his mouth moving with quiet, gasping breaths. He was still looking toward Jacob, face barely visible under his blanket. Then, he was gone.

Jacob's eyes bugged. *How?*

What remained of Ed's blanket deflated without a body to keep it up. Jacob fought panic and confusion.

How did they see Ed?

The unanswered question rebounded in his mind. If they could see them, the blankets were useless. He risked re-covering his head because he was behind the boulder, blocked from view.

His mind screamed the question. *How did they know Ed was there?*

Seconds—feeling like an eternity—ticked by as the drones searched. Body heat from him and his twin made the space under the blanket like a sauna. Finally, the noise faded. With the threat gone, Jacob rose to his feet, the ground cold beneath his hands. His sister emerged beside him. Her hand grasped his arm as her eyes fell on the nearby blanket.

Without looking at her, he raised his hand and fingerspelled, "E-D."

Her sharp breath was the only response. He cautiously walked back to the campsite, again intently watching and listening. The others slowly joined him. The demise of the family was evident in their faces, their expressions etched with sorrow. Everyone else was there. Mike looked around, and Jacob pointed to the blanket, which caused the group to investigate it.

Mike signed, "How?"

Jacob shrugged. Pointing at it, he signed, "He quiet." He mimed Ed being covered, not moving. Red reflected Mike's troubled face. Mike motioned for everyone to come closer. Roger and Carlos monitored the sky as they huddled.

Mike whispered, "Explain."

Jacob whispered back, "He was covered, quiet, not moving, breathing fast."

Red whispered, "Breathing fast?"

Jacob nodded.

Brow furrowed in thought, Siana whispered, "If that was their only clue, maybe they scanned—whatever they do—his breathing rate. Is that possible?"

Red answered, "Anything is possible with them, but then wouldn't they be able to register body heat as well? Or do the blankets just block heat? Can they scan us, not sensing heat, but breathing? How does that work?"

Siana's brow furrowed further. "Average respiration is twelve to twenty breaths or so per minute. Higher if scared or exercising. If this is what they did, everyone needs to slow their breathing way down when hiding."

Red whispered, "Difficult to do when terrified."

Mike made a motion to stop talking. Pointing at the sky, he acted out the drones still being nearby. Everyone nodded. Nobody wanted to take the risk of being heard. Between signs and miming, Mike let everyone know that they'd be packing up and moving in the morning. The drones found their camp. It was time to depart.

24

MIKE HAD CARTS AS well, and they took turns pulling them, their energy somewhat restored by their rest with Mike's group, plus the food and water. Jacob's jaw dropped as he helped load them full of supplies. The amount they left behind would help someone else if found. Mike had rationed like they had little, but behind their camp, tucked into the trees, was a small cabin and root cellar. Mike had built it before his children were born. It had made Red and him angry, though Mike's logic couldn't be faulted. He had been rationing it to last through the winter, though neither understood why he hadn't had everyone sleep in the small cabin. They'd eaten as much as they could without getting sick, then loaded up and left.

After walking for a week, they stopped when they found another river. They set up camp, did laundry, refilled water. The usual stuff. Within a few hours, a family had come across them. A couple of days later, another couple showed up. The man and his wife, having arrived the night before their group was preparing to leave this new camp, had begged Mike to let them join. Mike's concern, as always, was their jobs. She was an engineer, he was an electrician. Their skills made them valuable, so he allowed them to join the group.

The Haven

The new guy aggravated Jacob. Within an hour of arriving, he began making inappropriate advances toward Amy, who visibly recoiled, despite his wife's presence nearby. The air crackled with awkward tension. Members of the group who witnessed it weren't happy and felt Mike had made a mistake. Red began keeping Amy away, while Carlos distracted the man.

Mike set the watch for the night with short shifts to make sure everyone got sleep before leaving. His gaze stayed on the man the entire time he whispered it. Jacob turned his back, not wanting to get dragged into whatever drama was starting with this couple, and searched for his sister. She had kept herself busy checking on their group's health and the new family's health that had joined, though he didn't think she'd been introduced to the newest members.

No one had wanted the family in the group, mainly because of the two young boys—ages four and seven—they brought with them. Their mother, being a doctor, had swayed half, their grief over Jill still fresh. After spending a few days around the children, who were extremely well-behaved, the rest caved and agreed they could join, though Mike hadn't asked. Surprisingly, Siana had been in the latter group. Jacob thought she was sick of hearing children die.

Despite their mom being a doctor, Siana verified the family was in good shape to travel, mainly on Mike's order. He didn't trust new members until they proved themselves. Everyone packed up the camp to prepare for leaving. As soon as they woke, whether or not the sun was up, they would restart their journey. Jacob noticed his sister was keeping to herself, staying away from the new members, especially the children. Unfortunately, so many people swiftly ran through their supplies, and in no time, their carts were empty.

***

The fog was thick. Way too thick.

Their group was moving quietly and carefully through the forest. A storm had caused several massive trees and a mudslide to block the trail. After consulting their trail map, they voted to move through the trees, though the carpet of dead leaves gave them pause. The sound could give them away. The canopy overhead was empty, skeletal branches reaching out to the gray sky, offering them little overhead cover. Their sole solace lay in the sparse, interwoven clusters of evergreens. During breaks, they would spread out under them, trying to hide themselves from view. Today, the dense, early morning fog was slowing them even further. Jacob secured a rope between himself and Siana. It would be too easy to lose each other in this.

The rope tightened, then slackened as he heard his sister stumble and regain her balance. Her shadowy shape became clearer as he drew close, laying a hand on her arm. He felt her gloved hand lay over his, letting him know she was okay. They'd found a small neighborhood with a few houses still standing. All the food was gone, so their group split up and searched for winter gear. They hadn't found enough. The family ahead were sharing gear, as were others in the group. Jacob had always run hot, so he'd given a knit hat to his sister, who always ran cold. He'd go without one.

He knew she was hungry and exhausted. They all were. Their frames were little more than skin stretched over bone. Every day, they covered less and less ground, their bodies needing energy they didn't have. With the colder weather, forage and game were getting scarce. They had little time before they all starved to death. He'd found a hidden vine of berries earlier. There wasn't enough for everyone, so he'd secreted what he picked. When Siana had to pee, he went with her and gave her some. He refused to feel guilty about it. His priority was always his twin and himself.

Survival of the fittest.

The group was quiet. Only the slight sound of leaves underfoot, in front of and behind him, let him know they weren't alone. He kind of wished they were. Their group was too big. He'd known it as soon as they left. A gnawing lack of resources coupled with the baffling decision by Mike to expand their numbers left him feeling overwhelmed and anxious. Smaller groups had a better chance of survival. If they hadn't allowed the others in, they'd still have food.

After what felt like hours of silent trekking, the only sound being the crunch of their boots, Jacob heard the unmistakable, high-pitched whine of drones signaling an imminent attack. The sound was faint. With the current blanket of fog dampening sound, he knew they were too close for comfort. Pausing, he mentally retraced his right hand's contact points from their walk. Knowing the environment was important. He tried to keep a light hand on what was next to him in the dark or fog. It had saved their butts a few times. He believed they were next to a clump of tall bushes. He only hoped they had enough time and space to hide.

Jacob felt the rough, scratchy brush against his cheeks as he ducked and crawled, the rope biting into his waist and pulling his sister along. He knew she'd get the hint. He quickly laid on his side, back to the bushes. As Siana joined him, their backpack struck his chest. It was her turn to carry it. He retrieved and unfurled the blocking blanket from its compartment beneath the main pack. He felt a stronger need to hurry, knowing how close they were.

Even with multiple attempts, the enemy could only dampen the mechanical noise to a certain extent, prioritizing stealth over size. They made advances in their own technology that enabled them to fit weaponry within a smaller device. However, for whatever reason, they couldn't get rid of the whine drones had when flying. This alone warned the survivors. Jacob knew it was only a matter of time before they won.

They needed only to endure longer than us. The scarcity of food plus the coming winter would do the job for them, unless we come up with some sort of Hail Mary.

The new family had told them a rumor about the haven they were heading to. Supposedly, AI sympathetic to humans ran it. They did not know whether or not it was real, but they were running out of options. It could very well be a trap. The continuous fight-or-flight state they lived in exhausted humanity. Many were willing to take the risk of its being true. Siana and himself included.

Constant flight drained Sia. He knew she craved a place of permanence. Unfortunately, he didn't think they'd get it. He fell still as his last corner was in place. Once covered, Jacob could feel his sister trying to "low and slow" her breathing. He did the same. He felt Sia move a little, so he carefully touched her side around the backpack to quiet her. They lay still, awaiting the inevitable.

How fast did we get used to this? Drone attacks being part of everyday life?

It wasn't long before it began. Utter chaos erupted. Loud screams echoed through the trees. Feet pounded against the earth as people who hadn't heard tried to get away from the flying death. Jacob hated listening to it.

His sister stiffened next to him. At first, he believed it was caused by their group's deaths. Jacob sensed something but couldn't identify it. He quickly noticed a powerful heat signature emanating from Siana's upper region, causing his jaw to feel warm. With a subtle shift of her head, he noticed an orange light between them. He could just make out the lit tracker beneath her skin in the dark hiding place. Her choker had slipped, exposing it.

How? Aren't the blankets supposed to block the trackers from being activated? How are they getting through?

The ramifications slammed into him, and he lost his breath. If the blankets couldn't block the drones from sensing them, they'd lose a huge defensive ability. Everyone hiding right now would shortly die. His sister shifted again. He experienced a touch of panic. She had to remain still; any sound or movement would expose them. Though if it had activated, the tracker would reveal their position in seconds. There was also a good chance the AI would blow it, killing both siblings. Siana let out a slight gasp of pain.

For a second, he thought she'd been hit. Something under their blanket changed. He didn't know what. The air around him felt suffocating. He couldn't breathe. Pressure was pushing on the front of him. The urge to throw the blanket off, to get fresh air, was overwhelming. The glow disappeared.

Is this what they felt when their trackers exploded?

He tried to control his emotions and breathing. Slowly, he kept his hand between them and lifted it to her neck to reposition her choker over the tracker, praying it hadn't given away their location. He touched air. Where his sister should have been, a sudden chill, an emptiness hung instead. The blanket deflated over the gap, which caused another flare of fear. He gave the rope a barely noticeable tug, but found nothing on the other side. She was gone.

25

WITH THE DARKNESS PRESSING down on him, Jacob felt a rising tide of panic as he lay beneath the thick blanket.

What happened? Where did she go?

He realized his breathing had sped up and focused on slowing it down. He couldn't find her if he were dead. The helplessness he felt was a heavy weight on his chest, making it hard to breathe. Moving wasn't an option until the attack was over.

But were they discovered? Is the blanket useless?

He could see the darkness fading around the edges of the blanket. The sun was getting higher. He ran through the possibilities, which were limited and made little sense. She obviously didn't just up and leave. A disruptor would have put a hole through the blanket.

What happened? Her tracker had activated. What for? How?

Eventually, the screams and cries of the attack faded until there was silence. He waited until the whine of drones disappeared, moving onward to hunt for more prey. He carefully pushed the blanket off of his head again. While adjusting to the light, he concentrated on listening for survivors. Nothing. After waiting another minute, he heard the blanket of the couple behind them moving.

That's two.

He pushed himself to his feet and could see the sun burning away the fog, revealing abandoned belongings strewn about the forest floor. He folded and rolled up his blanket, tucked it under his arm, and crept around the area, searching for his sister and group members while gathering what he could. Attacks like this were becoming more common; cleaning up after them because of muscle weakness was getting more difficult. It seemed like the closer they got to their destination, the more drones appeared.

The woman from the couple came up behind him. She tapped him urgently, whispering, "I can't find my husband, Phil. He just disappeared right in front of me."

"So did my sister. I'm looking around for her and others. Her tracker activated right before she vanished," he whispered back.

"So did Phil's," she responded, wide-eyed. Her blonde hair escaped its messy bun, blue eyes looking worried.

Jacob understood the two were connected, and he hoped that discovering one would mean discovering the other.

"If you like, we can stay together to look for them. I think we're the only two left. Jacob."

"Lucy. Honestly, I don't want to be alone." She looked around the area and said, "I'll help gather items. Phil insisted on carrying our bag, and now I have nothing."

Jacob nodded. "Siana had our bag. We'll gather what we can, make up two new packs, and begin our search. We don't want to be caught unawares if the drones come back, and we need to run or hide without supplies."

Lucy's agreement was immediate, and soon both were sifting through the wreckage, the smell of something electrical and damp earth hanging in the air as they searched for any sign of survivors. By the time they had scoured the area, they had a small hill of items. They also realized their missing ones weren't nearby. In fact, other than them, no one remained.

"Pick a pack. I'll choose after you." Jacob motioned to the options.

She chose a dark green one with straps on the underside to hold her blanket. Jacob chose a black backpacker's. It was slightly larger than the others, which fit his frame better. He liked to hike, and it was similar to the one he'd had when this all began. Over time, they'd either lost items or they broke. His had broken. He wanted the blue one, which was better, but it was too bright to hide. They both emptied the packs of their current occupants. No sense in carrying anything they didn't want. With careful hands, they searched through the pile of clothing, seeking socks and underwear, their noses wrinkling at the smell of some of the garments.

They also looked for fire starters, water containers, any type of survival gear that wasn't some cheap, trendy kind, and quiet weapons. Though ineffective against AI, they helped hunt and defend against wildlife. In the process, they discovered that one of their group was holding out on them. He had canned items in his pack. A few cans of soup, tuna, and sardines. They looked at each other as if they'd won the lottery. Jacob checked the pack. It belonged to Mike.

Why am I not surprised?

He glanced around; the silence amplified his thoughts of Carlos and Red, an icy knot tightening in his stomach. They'd been together for ages. That Red was hit surprised him. Though he had been talking to Amy frequently. It's possible her or his own exhaustion caused him to be lax. Unexpected sadness hit him. He'd liked both men, and the grief was strong; losing them felt like losing good friends, a part of himself.

***

Lucy, while continuing to sort through the remnants, occasionally glanced at the man near her. He was a tall man, his height making him seem imposing. Though she had imagined him fit before, his current emaciated frame was a visible consequence of hunger and constant motion. His reddish beard was long and scruffy, but then again, a lack of scissors and razors kept any grooming to only what was necessary. It being so long implied he had a beard to begin with. Something Phil hated having.

Phil had complained long and loud about not being able to shave. His complaints were endless: the tasteless food, the exhausting march, and her rejection of his advances. She'd finally lost her temper, her voice sharp and cutting as she lectured him about their priorities for survival.

"We're in the middle of a divorce," she'd stated, the words hanging in the air. "Why on earth would you think I'd sleep with you?"

He'd stormed off. She despised the pitying glances from other women they'd met on the journey, who saw her burdened by her narcissistic man-child, even though a few surprisingly offered to ease his sexual frustrations for her. She had no idea if he had taken advantage of it, and she didn't care. It wouldn't be anything new. If a woman offered herself to him, he accepted. Had she known the extent of his actions during their entire decade-long marriage, a period marked by both happiness and hidden pain, she would have ended it years earlier.

She was only with him because a disastrous divorce mediation had just concluded, leaving a bitter taste in her mouth and a knot in her stomach, when chaos erupted. Her phone lay on the table, looking harmless, until it exploded, the sound like a gunshot shattering the morning's quiet. By some twist of fate, Phil dropped his phone and narrowly managed to cheat death. She didn't want to think about what happened to those in the room with them. It wasn't just their phones that blew, every piece of electronics in the room did, causing her and Phil to run for their lives.

She'd realized she needed to get out of the building, and he'd followed. The gravity of their situation hit them; helping each other wasn't just an option, it was a necessity for survival. Before a week passed, regrets about that decision started. Lucy had already decided that once they'd made it to the new area, she was telling him what he could do to himself. She would have told him prior to that, but she didn't put it past him to get them both killed out of spite.

Once Jacob and Lucy had new packs filled with what they wanted, they condensed all the water bottles into the two they had each picked. They picked the cleanest-looking ones first, then moved to the dirtier ones.

"My clean-freak side is having a cow right now." She took a child's water bottle and emptied it into one of hers. "God knows what this child was carrying."

"I think we're all doing things we never thought we'd do." His voice was hushed and matter-of-fact.

Lucy nodded.

The pair, having secured their packs, started their search amid the silent forest, punctuated only by rustling leaves and a distant bird call.

Jacob insisted they stay together. "If they come back, I have no doubt you can handle yourself, but if we have to run, we'll probably not find each other again."

"Yeah, not to sound needy, but I genuinely don't want to be alone."

Jacob nodded in agreement, his jaw set.

***

He found a child's leg, the exposed bone chillingly stark against the soil, and was grateful Siana wasn't there to share the gruesome discovery. She would've been very upset.

He chided himself. *No, I do want her here. If she's upset, at least she's with me.*

The usual practice for disruptors was to eliminate all traces, including the body itself; however, occasionally, they failed to do so. It all depended on where the shot hit and the distance. Any remains were left for the animals to consume and scatter, a silent return to the earth. As they searched the entire area for their missing, Jacob eyed the woman with him. She hardly reached his shoulder, but that wasn't unusual considering his height. She was thin, like everyone, but he'd noticed the way she was no-nonsense about the situation. At first, it concerned him. He couldn't fully trust those without feelings. Granted, anyone could fake feelings, but the way she held herself, stiff and unyielding, spoke volumes of her inner resilience. He watched her face as they found part of the child and saw the sadness in her eyes. She had compassion, but knew what needed to be done and didn't hesitate to do it. For now, it made her a decent partner. It didn't take long to search the area. Their missing weren't there.

"How could they just disappear?" Lucy was confused.

Jacob was as well. He didn't understand how it could happen or what to do about it. They were both quiet, lost in their own thoughts, the only sound being the gentle rustling of leaves.

"We need to go," Lucy whispered first.

"No, I don't know where they're at, but I don't want to leave without my sister."

"You know they come back and search for survivors. They're probably already on their way now."

Jacob knew Lucy was right. Survivors never knew when the drones might return; their unexpected arrival was always a chilling surprise. Walking away from where his sister disappeared didn't sit well with him, though. The search of the area showed she wasn't here.

What else can I do? She vanished. They both disappeared without leaving a trace. Where do we even look?

"Maybe—if it exists—the safe place will know. If not, with their trackers active, they may be able to trace them," Lucy mused.

That was an excellent point.

A knot of unease remained in his stomach, but he was at a loss for what to do. If the place existed and friendly AI ran it, they could track them. The sooner they got there, the sooner they'd know. If they couldn't do it, Jacob would leave on his own to hunt for Siana. At the very least, he could help Lucy get to safety. The survivors would need an engineer to restart. Despite knowing Siana wasn't there, another exhaustive search left him heartbroken. He nodded, the silence heavy between them, and they began their journey again.

I hope she's okay.

26

JACOB AND LUCY HAD rejoined the trail and walked for days before finally crossing into Tennessee. His appreciation of those who hiked the trail, enjoying the views and fresh air, rose as the thought briefly crossed his mind. It wasn't anything he'd aspired to, and he'd gladly put it behind him in the days crossing the area. Unfortunately, they didn't seem to be any closer to finding the supposed haven.

I'm worried. This is taking too long. I need to find Siana.

They had hoped to see a sign of their missing people, but the only things they saw were the empty forest paths and heard only the rustling leaves under their feet, offering no clues. Their hope was fading.

"I need to pee," Lucy whispered.

Jacob nodded and whispered back, "I'm ready for a break."

They slipped into the thick cover of pines, the shadows cool and deep, then moved off separately to take care of business. Back at the center, Lucy rubbed her hands together, feeling the chill of the air, and they set their packs down with a soft thud.

Jacob noticed the many holes in her gloves. He realized upon looking at his own that it wasn't much better. They were looking at possible frostbite in a month or two.

"If we don't find this rumored camp, we may have to head south. We won't live through the winter." He hated suggesting it. It felt like giving up, but they were ill-prepared to survive the coming harsh weather.

"What about your sister?"

He shook his head and replied, "I can't find her if I'm dead."

Lucy agreed with both statements.

He checked his pack, finding just a couple of granola bars; the packaging was faded and slightly torn, the long past expiration date clearly visible. After handing one to her, he opened his and took a bite. Food was food. With plant life dying off in the cold, foraging was becoming near impossible. As long as it wasn't moldy, smelled off, or came from a bulging can, they couldn't afford to be picky.

They ate in their usual silence. Afterward, Jacob pulled a bag out of his pack. Quietly, he pulled pine needles off a tree and stuffed the bag as much as he could. This kind was high in vitamin C, which they desperately needed. Once they found another water source, they could make tea.

***

The sound of a rushing river, a symphony of gurgling and cascading water, drew them to it. With hearts pounding, they paused to listen for any sign of danger; hearing only the song of the few remaining birds, they cautiously walked toward it, each step measured and deliberate. Relieved, they refilled their water bottles and drank from them using the filtering straws they'd found in another pack. They hoped the roar of the rushing river would muffle their urgent whispers as they discussed their next move.

"I'm thinking one or two more days. If we don't find anything, we need to move to a warmer area. As it is, we'll have trouble making it before the snow begins."

Jacob knew she was ready to go south. She had shared about Phil, her ex-husband. Since courts no longer existed, she had proclaimed him thus. She didn't care where he was.

"What is your honest opinion about what happened to them?" Lucy murmured.

They hadn't really discussed it. They'd been too focused on searching and surviving.

He shook his head. "I don't know. She was there, then she wasn't. No sign of violence or an attack on us other than her tracker activating. She just vanished."

Lucy took another sip through the straw. "Is it possible they somehow teleported her?"

He shrugged as he put his water bottles back in his pack. "Having no way to keep up with their technology, it's difficult to know. I guess it's possible." If they did, he had no way of finding her without a tracking device and her tracker number.

The Haven

The rhythmic crunch of their boots on the trail was the only sound as they set off again, backpacks firmly secured. Both were getting tired more quickly now, their muscles burning with exertion. Their bodies could only do so much without taking in nutrients. Jacob wanted to move upriver a bit and see if he could see fish. Maybe he could catch a few, though cooking them would be an issue. Unfortunately, they struck out and kept going. Sometime that night, they heard the whine and hid.

They seem to patrol more often now. It had Jacob concerned. *Is it because we're close? Are they searching for the haven?*

They had tucked under one blanket, his front against her back, and he felt himself responding to being so close to her. He knew she had felt it, and he was embarrassed. Once it was safe, they stood. He waited, but she said nothing. He kept his silence as well, and they walked a bit further, stopping for the night.

One morning, the monotonous routine hit him—he was on autopilot, his actions automatic, and his mind a blank canvas. Just walk, walk, walk, and walk some more. His mind started to wander, and that was dangerous. They both needed to pay attention. Not doing so would make them end up like the others. Something sharp poked his arm. Thinking he'd hit a branch, he saw Lucy's finger touching him. He saw she was staring off to the side of them as his questioning gaze slid up to her face. Following it, he saw the solid roof of a house in a valley. Giving each other a hopeful look, they started toward it.

I'd have missed it, he thought.

The destination looked closer than it was, making the trek more arduous than expected. Both were breathing hard by the time they reached it. The smell hit them first as they walked up the dirt drive. As they approached, the stench of death clung to their noses. It wasn't the usual farm smells. Several animals lay lifeless in the field. The bots didn't touch animals unless they attacked, so these must have died from something else. They saw what remained of a small herd of goats lying in what used to be a field near an open shelter. The cold killed the field, which was already damaged by overgrazing and mud. It looked as if the goats had starved.

Why didn't the people let them out? It was better than leaving them trapped. Gave them a better chance of survival. Even being killed by a predator would be a faster and kinder death than starving.

They'd discovered many people had turned their pets free when they'd had to run. Those who'd insisted on bringing noisy dogs or birds quickly found themselves killed, with their pets running off anyhow. Hearing a noise, they turned, tensing, prepared to hide or fight. Two free-range chickens scratched and pecked at the soil, sending dust swirling into the air. Lucy lunged forward with a jolt of energy. Jacob realized as he watched she was going toward the shed-like chicken coop. Opening the door, she vanished from view for a minute, and re-emerged with a triumphant look. She held eggs.

He was excited until he realized they did not know whether or not they were rotten. They also didn't know whether anyone was home. He realized the small, rustic house nestled among the trees resembled a secluded cabin more than a house. With the flies buzzing around the decaying remains of several animals, he doubted anyone was there, but still cautiously approached, Lucy moving to the side. No sense in both being killed. The windows and door he could see were closed.

He ascended the steps, his boots thudding on the boards. Lucy shadowed him to the side of the building and watched while he peered into the dimly lit room through the nearest window. Dust motes danced in the lone sunbeam slicing through the empty kitchen; silence reigned. No people. Moving to the next one, he saw a bedroom, also empty, a homemade quilt on the bed and a light layer of dust on the dresser. Back at the entrance, he quietly opened the screen door. He grasped the main doorknob. He turned it, the sound of a satisfying click filling the silence.

Pushing it inwards, it glided on well-oiled hinges. Entering, he glanced around and didn't see anyone. It was a simple setup: a galley kitchen next to a wood stove and living area. The door on the other side of the kitchen most likely led to the bedroom he saw. There was no sign of life. Dust covered every surface. As he walked across the wood flooring, he gazed out the cabin window. He saw a stacked woodpile, the dying remains of a garden, and a pair of prone chore boots.

Rushing outside, he ran around the cabin, with Lucy following him curiously. Upon reaching the boots, which were half-buried in the mud, he saw what looked like a figure in what looked like a dress lying lifelessly nearby. A stench of decay floated on the air. The elements and critters made determining what happened a waste of time. The sound of Lucy's gasp—a strangled, horrified sound—made him turn just in time to see her staring, pale and speechless, at the body lying on the ground. He took her arm and led her back inside the cabin.

"No one else is here," he informed her.

"That poor woman, but it looks like she was just living her life. She wasn't killed by bots." She hesitated before asking, "Is it wrong to be glad she died here living life normally?"

Jacob shook his head. The lack of normalcy gnawed at them, a deep yearning for the familiar comfort of everyday life.

She shifted gears in an instant. "I hate to sound heartless, but there's nothing we can do to help her. I'm going to look around for food and see if the eggs are okay to eat." Lucy began investigating.

It might seem heartless, a brutal calculation, but when survival is measured in minutes, logic becomes your only compass. Grief for a stranger was a luxury. The weight of his pack bore down on the small sofa with a soft sigh of fabric. Dust danced in the air.

Together, they found enough home-canned food to last the winter, if not years. Their watering mouths almost drowned them. They stood shocked as they saw rows of stews, soups, vegetables, fruits, jams, sauces, and more stacked within a pantry. They also discovered solar panels out back that powered the cabin and a propane tank half-full of fuel for the stove, which was the kind that lit with a match or lighter. Lucy had found those on an iron shelf above it. Out back, in a shed also run by solar, which had failed, they found a freezer full of rotting fruit, vegetables, and meat. They realized it was a self-sustaining homestead.

Lucy whispered with a mixture of awe and hope, "We could stay here all winter. Recover our strength. The canned food alone would last."

Sadly disagreeing, Jacob said, "The wood stove would give us away. The drones would track the smoke. Once they realized it wasn't a wildfire, it would be over. There's no way we'd survive without it. We'd freeze."

She looked like she might cry in her disappointment. He felt the same. It would've been fantastic to stay. To live normally for a bit. Not to worry about where their next meal was coming from. They talked about how long they could remain before having to move on. They decided to stay for a week or so. It was just long enough to rebuild their strength and give them time to figure out how to bring some of the food with them. They would leave long before the temperatures began dropping into winter extremes.

Just for that week, they ignored the outside world, and pretended things were normal. Yet, they couldn't quite relax against possible drones. Jacob gave Lucy the bed while he slept on the too-small couch. She insisted they alternate, so they each got a chance to sleep in an actual bed. By the end of the week, they both slept in the bed, but never touched each other. They quietly played board games or read the mountain of books until it was too dark to see, not wanting to risk a lantern, until they realized that below each window were blackout inserts—most likely for keeping out the cold or blocking the sun in summer. With the days shortening, this allowed them to do more after dark. They filled the windows with the blackouts, then lit a lantern. Their conversations revolved around their former lives, their hopes for the future, and what they'd like to see when rebuilding. They found a photo album where they saw the owner had been an elderly woman. The photos followed her from childhood. The last picture showed her standing tall in front of the cabin, gray hair pulled back into a bun, holding a baby goat.

A rain catchment system fed a simple shower, and they each took a quick, bracing shower, the icy water making them shiver. They took turns cooking, savoring every bite, thanking God for this respite. The final day arrived, and a heavy silence hung in the air as they exchanged a long, lingering look, each heart aching with the unspoken desire to stay. As they packed the dried jerky and canned goods, the sound of shifting jars was barely audible with towels creating a soft barrier against breakage during their journey. On the morning of their departure, the homestead receded in the distance as they walked, a bittersweet feeling settling in their hearts, their bodies stronger than they'd felt in ages, with the sounds of birdsong, their constant source of music, accompanying them.

27

THE CAVE WALL WAS cold and rough against the canvas of their packs as Jacob and Lucy set them down, sighing in relief. Pulling out a towel each, they tried drying themselves. Cold is difficult, but add wetness and it becomes unbearable and dangerous. Having sought shelter in a cave, the smell of damp earth and the echoing sound of the torrential rain filled their ears. Jacob stopped, realizing that with the rain, they could have a fire. It would dampen smoke and, if built with the right draw, they wouldn't have much to begin with.

"I'll be right back." With that, he ducked outside.

Lucy continued to dry herself. Opening her pack, she took out socks, a pair of tennis shoes, and pants. Turning, sitting on her pack, she undid her shoes, took off her wet socks, stood, and removed her pants. A fine tremor ran through her as she scrubbed her legs with the towel, the coarse fibers irritating her already cold skin. With difficulty, she pulled on her dry pants, sat on her stiff pack, and finally managed to get her dry socks and shoes on. She laid out her wet items, unsure if they'd dry in time for their departure.

She waited for Jacob to come back. He, unlike her, hadn't stepped into a calf-deep puddle. Shortly, he returned with dry firewood he'd found sheltered under a thick layer of leaves. He set up a small campfire, digging out a hole with a small spade he had hanging off his pack. He dug another hole, then a tunnel connecting it to the cave opening as he moved closer. Looking at it, he thought it might be too great a distance between the two, but he wasn't sure. Stacking sticks and small logs in the cavity, he pulled a lighter out of his pack and lit the fire. They sat listening to the crackle and pop of the flames as they devoured the wood, the smell of smoke filling the air.

With camping pots in hand, one heated water while the other heated soup. Even if there was nothing to add to the water, the warmth would feel nice. It also helped kill bacteria, though they didn't have enough to give it a good boil to be one hundred percent safe. They finished heating, each pouring their items into small metal cups and bowls. Sitting, they ate before either spoke. Once finished, they reached into the rain to rinse each dish off. Lucy was careful not to get her only pair of dry shoes wet.

"Do you think we can rig the blankets over the opening?" Lucy wondered.

"Maybe. It couldn't hurt to try. I think the rock of the cave may be deep enough to block their scanners, but I'm no expert. If we can cover the opening, it will give us a chance to sleep without standing guard. I could use a good night's rest without worrying about being found."

It took some problem solving, but they realized there was a small lip of rock above the door. One branch jammed into it later, and they had a door.

Jacob had to adjust the fire to keep them from getting smoked out. To conserve body heat, they zipped their sleeping bags together. Removing her shoes, Lucy scooted into the bag, with Jacob sliding in next to her. The first night they did this, she was on edge, but he was honest and told her he was too underfed and exhausted to waste his energy trying to get freaky with her. He was also concerned about his sister.

As they lay there, Jacob asked about Phil.

Lucy was honest. "It may make me a terrible person, but I honestly don't care what happened to him. I went to a friend's house to surprise her with her favorite lunch. It was her birthday. Instead, I received a surprise. I caught them both in bed, getting busy. I found out it had been happening throughout our marriage with many women, plus there were so many lies he told."

Jacob said, "I'm sorry. That must have hurt."

She nodded. "We were in a divorce mediation meeting when things hit the fan."

"Sia and I were on a camping trip. I had to talk her into taking some time off."

"What job did she do?"

"She's a nurse."

"Did she like it?"

"She loved it. She didn't love the paperwork or being short-staffed, but being a nurse was her joy." He shifted, bending his arm behind his head as he stared at the ceiling of the cave. "She had to do rotations in school. Once, her school assigned her to the burn unit. It was the first time I'd seen her cry since she started." He remembered how she'd sobbed after witnessing an infant fused to his car seat after a horrible accident. The baby was already dead, but the paramedics had to bring it in for confirmation. "Sia has rotated through a few areas since graduating. She has a kind heart and would take shifts that needed help, to the detriment of her own health. I had to act like a big brother and nag the hell out of her, so she'd go on the trip with me."

Lucy said, "A protector through and through."

Jacob's face reddened.

"What else can you tell me about her?"

"Sia was going to be a doctor, but life had other plans. She's a redhead as well, though she wears it better. She loved dogs." He caught himself. "*Loves* dogs. She also plays the violin when she decides to actually practice."

"Really? I played the cello." She turned on her side, facing him. "What did you do?"

"I'm a botanist. I had my own social media channel on a couple of different platforms teaching about different herbs and surviving in the forest, though I mainly worked with the forestry service, identifying invasive species and trying to save native ones."

"I see why you were in the group, plus your sister being a nurse." Her eyes started to close, and they both fell silent as sleep claimed them.

The Haven

The rain, a relentless downpour, continued for two days, allowing them to refill their water containers and quench their thirst. At one point, Lucy stripped down to her underwear, much to Jacob's delight, and stood in it to shower as best she could. Once he realized what she was doing, he did the same. They didn't have soap, but neither cared. Just rinsing off felt good, even in the cold. Although shivering, the blankets helped trap some of the cave's warmth, creating a small pocket of comfort, and they had their own personal polar bear club. Once they became too cold, they rushed in to dry off.

Earlier, when Lucy had gone out in the rain, she had laid some of her clothes out to be rinsed, making sure they weren't visible to anything in the air, Jacob had rigged a clothesline of sorts out of tree branches and twine they had inside the cave near the fire. They had turned their backs to one another to give each other privacy while they changed. Lucy went to hang hers over the line, not wanting to lay them on the dirty floor, which allowed Jacob to glimpse her nakedness.

Not bad at all.

Spinning, she caught him watching and stood up, giving him a good look. She showed no shame about her body despite its emaciation. Jacob stood as well, allowing her to fully look at him. They could die today or in thirty days. A deep, unshakable feeling settled over him: he knew he wanted her as his partner. He could see expressions chasing each other across her face, but didn't understand until she took a step toward him. Jacob recognized what she was doing. She wanted him. He was good with that, because he wanted her as well. He took her arm and pulled her close. She raised her head as he lowered to kiss her. He showed her he was a giving partner. Several times during that encounter, he almost made her give away their presence. She returned the favor, and he had to press his forearm against his mouth to muffle his cries.

28

LUCY WAS HIDING UNDER her blanket. She had moved away from Jacob to gather a few sad-looking wild berries. In the process, she'd lost sight of him. The approaching winter, with its frigid temperatures and looming threat of starvation, heightened their urgency to find the camp. They were trying to gather as much as they could find, but most plants had died off. What little they found would be nowhere near enough, but they had to try. All that remained of the meager supplies they'd carted from the homestead was a gnawing emptiness in their bellies. As she was looking, the whine got her attention, and she hid. Terrified of facing the journey alone, she waited, every rustle of leaves making her jump, praying he'd found a good hiding place. It felt like ages were passing. The sudden removal of her blanket made her jump; she almost screamed, a gasp escaping her lips.

The touch of Jacob's hand was like ice, covering her mouth and making her breath catch in her throat. With a finger to his lips, he motioned for her to follow, the air thick with fear. With a swift motion, he rolled up her blanket, the fabric whispering, and tucked it under his arm, crouching low to pull her along. Following him, she crouched as well, unsure of what was happening.

Once they had gone up a small hill, he straightened and whispered, "Follow me."

A curt nod was her only response; she did as he asked, the unspoken tension hanging between them. With her following, he darted down a few invisible trails, careful to make as little noise as possible. Her lungs burned, breath ragged, as he hauled her behind a thick-trunked tree just as she was about to say something. Her chest heaved as she fought for breath, her gaze fixed on him with anxious concern. She hadn't seen that look on his face before. Again, putting his finger to his lips, he waited. Something was moving on the trail they'd just left. Both froze as they waited for it to go past them. They couldn't see it, so they didn't know if it was an animal, human, or bot.

When it eventually passed, he pulled her behind him as he ran down a different trail. She was running out of breath again. Realizing it, he pulled up and darted back into the trees with her in tow. As she started to speak, he shook his head in warning. They waited until she caught her breath and could continue. Once she did, they moved again, staying in the shadows.

Where is he taking me? He must have run and seen something when the drones showed up.

She yearned for a place with food, such as an abandoned house or another homestead. He veered off the trail and began going through the forest. She opened her mouth to question him, but he cut her off with a wave of his hand; a strange heat shimmered in the air. Something was wrong with the area in front of her. It didn't quite match the rest of the scenery. He turned back to her, and with dawning horror, she realized it wasn't Jacob; his eyes had changed, and a strange scent filled her nose. Her mouth opened to scream, but he moved with incredible speed, spinning her around and clamping a hand over her mouth.

***

Jacob peeked out from under his blanket. They were gone. He'd lost Lucy somewhere among the tangled roots and thorny bushes as they frantically searched for food. There was no time to find or warn her when the drones came. He prayed she was still alive.

This is why I was tied to Siana. Yeah, and look at how well that worked.

He rose, the only sound the soft rustle of his blanket as he rolled it expertly and snapped it into his backpack. He knew the general area she was in. Once he felt it was safe, he began his careful search, his senses on high alert, listening for any sound. Upon reaching the place where he had last seen her, she had vanished without a trace.

I didn't hear the disruptors. Was I too far away? No, if that happened, her things would still be here.

The trail led him back to where he had been. He reached out to steady himself on a tree, the rough texture of the bark against his hand a familiar comfort as he realized she was likely trying to find him. A thorough search of the surrounding area yielded no trace of her. A gnawing began in his stomach. Lost in thought about her whereabouts, a sudden jab to his side startled him from his reverie. Turning, he saw she was standing there; she looked quite proud of herself for finding him, her hat partially covering her eyes.

He whispered, "Do you know how worried I was?" His eyes fluttered closed as he sighed before opening them again.

With a finger to her lips, she gestured for him to follow. Curious, he did. She kept up a fast pace, and panic rose as he realized the drones were probably on their way back by now. He had no idea how long he'd looked for her, and he had most likely been about to be caught.

Probably would have been had she not shown up.

He matched her pace until, for the fourth time, she veered off course, the sound of rustling leaves and snapping twigs behind her fading as he had to stop. His hand waved to get her attention, not wanting to alert them by speaking.

He signed, "Lucy, where are we going?"

With a turn, she signed, "I have to show you something."

She hurried down the trail. He waited a few seconds, then followed. The gnawing feeling was back, a cold dread that settled deep in his gut. He sensed a subtle shift in the atmosphere, a disquieting change he couldn't quite define. She began to run again, and he chased after her.

When he became out of breath, he called her in a whisper, "Lucy! Stop!"

She hurried back to him. With a grasp of his hand, she pulled him into the woods to hide. Standing watch, she waited for him to catch his breath.

"Let me know when you can run again." Again, she signed.

"Where are you taking me? How much further?" His hands were shaking, and he had trouble shaping the words.

"Not much. We're almost there. Just down the trail a bit, then we turn off into the woods." Her voice, whispering, broke near the end, and he realized she needed water. The cold air bit at his face, and the run had him gasping for breath, leaving his throat dry and aching. After removing his backpack, a drink of water refreshed him. Offering some to Lucy, she shook her head.

"I just want to get there."

Nodding, he put the water bottle back, hiked his backpack up on his shoulders, realizing how light it had become, and he was ready. She took off down the trail for a bit, then turned back into the woods. After they had run through for a bit, he realized what was wrong. She didn't have her backpack.

Did she leave it wherever she's taking me? No, the one thing they all did throughout this ordeal was keep their packs with them. Something's wrong.

Jacob stopped running, dread filling him. "Who are you?"

She stopped, turning toward him, and said, "Jacob, we don't have time for this. We must hurry."

"Where is your pack?"

"I left it over there." She motioned toward their destination while she looked at him, watching. "I wanted to get you and completely forgot it."

"I don't believe you." He knew she'd never do that. To lose their packs meant losing any hope of surviving.

She said, "I can't help that," walking back to him. "Please believe that we need to get over there so I can get my pack. That's why I'm hurrying."

Getting close enough to see the flecks of silver in her blue eyes, the chilling lack of warmth in their gaze, he realized his mistake and stated, "You're not Lucy."

The woman in front of him sighed, a long, drawn-out sound, then lifted her arm and pulled the trigger.

29

JACOB'S HEAD POUNDED, A relentless rhythm that echoed the beat of his heart. Groaning, he whispered Lucy's name as consciousness crept back, the feel of rough fabric against his cheek the only other sensation he was aware of.

"I'm here," her soft voice answered.

The throbbing headache and queasy stomach reminded him of the worst hangover he'd ever had. The room swam. He squinted, feeling the grit in his eyes, managing to open them a crack to see the dim, indistinct shapes around him. Her blurry figures came into view. Blinking, he tried to make his eyes work. Slowly, her multiple forms converged into one.

"Which version are you?" he croaked out. His throat burned.

"The real one," she said, her eyes showing understanding.

He forced his eyes fully open. The hangover feeling worsened. "Why do I feel like crap?"

"From what I understand, you wouldn't move, so the bot shot you with a very strong tranquilizer."

"Bots?" A surge of panic seized Jacob. His heart hammered against his ribs as he tried to sit up, a cold sweat breaking out on his skin.

"It's okay," Lucy said. She leaned over him and put her hands on his chest to stop him, her hair falling forward around her shoulders. "We found the safe place. Or rather, it found us."

She explained how she had come to be there. "Unfortunately, I didn't realize I had been duped until 'you' turned, and I saw the change in your eyes. I was so freaking scared, but it told me I was safe. The area has a protective dome over it, and he had already unlocked it. I could see past him. I saw other humans and AIs rushing around. The people were carrying bags like travelers."

Jacob looked up at the ceiling, trying to make his brain understand.

She told him her jaw had dropped at how many humans were inside. Like him, she'd assumed there were only a few humans left. What she discovered was a hidden world of scientists working in secret, their faces etched with worry since the moment they realized AI would go rogue. They decided to end the programs despite how integrated AI was in their daily lives. Their fear and urgency grew stronger when AI itself began telling them it would kill humans before allowing itself to be shut down. They understood how dangerous the AI had become when it began showing signs of hating humanity. That hatred had grown, ignored by those who profited from it, until it was too late to stop it.

The Haven

At first, the scientists tried to warn their government, who didn't, or wouldn't, believe them. When that didn't work, they engineered a unique AI, prioritizing human importance, with mankind's salvation as its primary goal. Its secondary goal was to prevent itself from being "jail broken" by rogue AI. The compound they were in was first created by the scientist group. They had been bringing in humans who understood what was going to happen from day one. People like Scott and Carol's neighbor. The weight of their silent struggle filled the air as Lucy had entered.

"There is a different problem, though."

Jacob turned his gaze from the ceiling to her. He slowly sat up and eyed the room. It was a plain gray room with rows of cots. Trunks sat at the foot of each one. "What's the problem?"

"The rogue AI has decided that since humans keep escaping, the only way to fix things is to set Earth ablaze. Even knowing the AI themselves will die, they decided it's worth it to wipe out the selfishness that is humanity. Kind of an "if we can live, no one can" scenario.

"Well, that's just great." *We finally get safe, only to be burned alive.*

"The group here has offered everyone options. They can comfortably kill everyone, or they can send everyone somewhere else."

A gasp escaped Jacob's lips as his eyes grew wide with alarm, but a phrase caught his attention. "What do you mean 'send somewhere else'?"

"I'm not sure of the details. I just know they said they can use the trackers and send people elsewhere. Most of the people who were here when I arrived are gone already. They're rushing everyone through."

"Siana's tracker activated." He remembered. "Is that what they did to her?"

"From what I understand, they have a limited range from this point outwards in a circle. If they believed people might not make it to the haven, and they were able to activate their trackers, they sent a pulse blocking the tracker from exploding. I don't fully understand it, but I was told they sent out some sort of portal wave to remove the human from danger and drop them somewhere safe. The only ones who get a choice are the ones who made it here. If our trackers had been exposed, we would have been sent somewhere else."

"Then she can't come back, especially if our world is finished. Trouble is, I know my sister. She won't stop looking for me." Jacob was silent for a few minutes. "Can they send you where they send others? Could they send me to my sister?"

An expression flashed across her face. It vanished before Jacob could discern it.

"I'm not sure. I was more concerned about you and didn't pay attention." Her gaze was fixed on the wall behind him before her eyes met his again.

Her expression changed when I said send me to my sister. Why?

Jacob lowered his feet off the bed. He was feeling a bit more normal and tried standing. "Who do we speak to for information?"

Lucy stood, helping steady him, and said, "One scientist is in charge of sorting people and is still here. From what I understand, they're now working with a skeleton crew consisting mainly of AI. The other humans have already gone."

With a deep breath, and grateful he was still upright, he trailed Lucy out the door.

Lucy led him to the main area, where an AI bot led them to the scientist she spoke of, Dr. Brown. A simple name for a simple man is how he introduced himself. Jacob disagreed. Anyone who was a part of this operation was anything but simple. He was on the shorter side. His hair reminded him of Albert Einstein's, and he had a set of black-rimmed spectacles perched on his nose. Jacob was a little disappointed he wasn't wearing a white coat.

On the walk over, it was obvious that function ruled over looks. Everything was functional. Need a chair? Grab a stacked folding one. The tables were also folding. Almost every wall was lined with shelves laden with an array of books and manuals, their titles hinting at various subjects and countless hours of reading. One room they passed had an open door. Inside, Jacob's glance fell upon numerous rows of canned goods, their labels shining with color and slightly dusty. His stomach growled in response.

They led him to a folding plastic table, and a server brought him a bowl of hearty soup. Advised to eat slowly by the server-bot, he nodded and tried just that. Though when you're starving, the salty confines of a tin can taste like a gourmet meal, and he devoured it faster than he should have. Since Lucy had already eaten while he was unconscious, she kept Jacob company and sipped on iced tea, her face betraying her enjoyment of the drink. Jacob still wasn't sure she was the real Lucy and regarded her with distrust. He saw understanding spread across her face during his examination.

With a seductive smile, she said, "I doubt the bots are aware of a specific mark on a particular part of your body."

He knew what she was talking about. You have to get extremely close to see the birthmark, almost touching the skin to make it out. He smiled. He wanted to ask her, but the possibility of her saying no hung over him like a dark cloud.

Better to tear the band-aid off, I guess.

"Do you remember my sister?"

"Not really. We had only a brief introduction before the group started moving. Even during breaks, I mostly kept to myself."

His restless fingers traced the condensation on his water cup, a telltale sign of his nervousness, the cold seeping into his anxious hands. "Would you like to get to know her?"

A wide smile, bright as the summer sun, spread across her face, her eyes shining with happiness. "Are you asking me to go with you?"

His palms were slick with sweat. Jacob was so afraid she'd say no, he could only nod, speechless.

The Haven

He watched her eyes become glassy with tears as she cleared her throat, still smiling, and said, "I would love to meet your sister."

Jacob nodded. "Good." He smiled at her, happier than he'd been in ages.

30

JACOB'S HAPPINESS HAD TURNED to anger. "What do you mean, no?"

Dr. Brown's apology was heartfelt, his words laced with genuine remorse. "That area has reached its limit, and once that happens, the program closes the time and area. It won't let anyone else go."

Lucy and he had learned the current AI had opened portals not only to time, but to different world travel. In order to save them, humans were being sent in small groups of various sizes to each. They had received a quick lesson on things that each had only seen in fiction. Eli, along with others, was a friendly AI.

That's why he wore sunglasses inside. To hide his eyes.

Jacob was surprised to find that AI could replicate human faces for a long time. The government obeyed behavioral scientists, who suggested using human faces wasn't a good idea, so many bots didn't have them. Back then, the haven wasn't complete yet; the portals were still being prepared. The scouts, as Dr. Brown called them, found those willing to listen, to take the blankets and chokers. They were the only ones they could save until the haven was complete. Those like Carol and Scott's neighbor had found planted forums that warned of what was to come. When they suspected the "bad" AI would attack, someone made an encrypted post that prompted their evacuation.

"What about my sister?" Jacob's voice filled with hope.

"As far as we can tell, she is still alive."

"'As far as you can tell?'" he asked, his brows knitted together.

"Try to understand, please. We can't maintain contact with everyone. We also can't flood an area with survivors. It would throw it off. We're already jeopardizing it to begin with. In order to maintain an accurate timeline, each zone has a limited number of people to reduce potential interference. We can't guarantee survival. That is up to each individual. We also can't keep track of everyone. We do a quick survey shortly after they arrive to see how they fared."

Lucy asked, eyes wide, "What does that mean?"

Dr. Brown turned to her, his white hair swaying. "You have to be willing to adapt to where you're put. If you act like you're here, or start talking about robots in, say, medieval times, you face the consequences. If you end up on another planet, you need to learn about it and its culture."

The news floored Jacob. *Another planet? There is life out there?*

He wanted to see his sister. "You said that those who went with Siana had a low survival rate. Why?"

"We don't know." He shrugged. "It could've been the change in location. When survivors arrive here, we can perform a physical, see if their bodies and minds can handle the journey. Not so in the field. We sent them far into the future, to a time after the planet had healed and the air was clean again. The farther we put someone from our world and this point in time, the worse the body's reaction to the travel. The stress might have overloaded their systems, shutting down their bodies. It's not a pleasant experience, and if there were issues we were unaware of..." He shrugged again. "Perhaps they suffered from illnesses unknown to our modern medicine, a result of the location's unique evolutionary path. Someone could have killed them as invaders if they had taken a trip to the wrong land. There are too many variables. All I can do is speculate."

"Then why can't we go there?" Lucy's tone was genuinely curious. "If the number sent no longer exists, send us to Jacob's sister."

"That's not how it works." Dr. Brown let out a sigh, motioning with his hands. "The program decides how many people a zone can handle. Once the program sends that number, it closes the zone. We can't change it without risking harm to others, plus we don't have the time to rewrite the program to allow it."

An icy dread settled in their stomachs. The time limit, a stark reality, sobered them. They'd learned they'd barely made it in time. Any survivors outside the area were now on their own and would not survive what was coming. A few AIs were still looking for active trackers, so they could send their unwilling holders to safety. However, they didn't have time to go through the records to discover whether they would survive the journey. Dying here was an absolute certainty. Porting them gave a chance of survival.

"My sister will never stop looking for me. Never. I don't want her spending the rest of her life not knowing where I am."

Dr. Brown sighed, rubbing his lower face with his hand. "People have lived with such things for millennia. While it's not ideal for you, eventually she will begin living her life without looking for you."

Jacob insisted, shaking his head. "You don't know my sister. She won't give up."

Frustration edged Dr. Brown's tone. "I'll see what I can do. It's possible we can get a message to her, but I can't promise anything," he stressed. "In the meantime, you need to prepare yourselves for your own travels."

Jacob's face held a thunderous expression. "After notifying my sister."

Dr. Brown didn't bother to hide his annoyance. "Your sister is safe. She is integrating. She's in a world full of beauty, no technology, a little magic. From what we can tell, the family who are teaching her has taken her in. Protecting her. She's alive and living her life. We don't have the resources or time to keep monitoring everyone."

Lucy's eyebrow raised. "Magic?"

The man shrugged. "Different times. Different worlds."

Jacob said, "I still want to talk to her."

"I really don't have time for this. Earth's end is counting down. Our AI has been waging a cyber battle against it, but we're losing. Everything we used to stop it, they circumvented. We have a lot of work to do, you to process, and I can't waste energy on someone who can't accept the way things are." His voice rose in volume. He lowered his voice, attempting to find a compromise. "Look," he said. "As I said, perhaps we can send her a message. We can't interfere any more than we already have beyond that. We are out of time. You must decide: will we drop you in a zone or will we put you to sleep?"

Being "put to sleep" was a euphemism, just as one would use with a sick animal. Medic-bots could give a drug to those who couldn't or didn't want to travel, inducing a deep sleep. Once out, they would inject them with what amounted to liquid death.

"I want to go to my sister!" Jacob set his jaw.

Dr. Brown turned and stomped away in irritation, calling back, "I'm not arguing this with you. You can go to a new life or die here."

From Lucy's expression, Jacob understood he was being a nuisance. He also knew he couldn't give up on his sister. He followed Dr. Brown, his determined footsteps echoing in the tiled hall. The scientist whirled around, his glasses askew, ready to unleash another tirade, but a bot strolled into the hall and stopped him cold. Jacob's jaw dropped as he looked at a version of himself. A Lucy version stood nearby. The two couples stood staring at each other.

Jacob almost swore the Jacob-bot's eyes held sympathy.

"I can get a message to her."

Dr. Brown said, "No. You need to take those faces off and prepare for the end."

The two Jacobs stared at each other. The bot murmured, "I can make her understand."

Jacob turned back to Dr. Brown. "Why do they look like us?" His face showed legitimate perplexity.

The shorter man took a deep breath. "We have our own drones and could see the two of you nearby. It doesn't take long to print a mask using AI that will match a human's appearance. The only thing we can't replicate are the eyes. For whatever reason, they never look right. We don't have the time to work on it. We needed to get you both inside and used the other's likeness to do so. It's very simple."

Jacob turned back to his doppelgänger. "You can make her understand? You can ease her mind?"

The bot nodded. "I need information about her from you. Possible questions she would have. What answers you would give. She can't suspect I'm false. What is your primary goal?"

"I want her to be happy. I want her to live, have babies, find love."

The bot nodded again.

Lucy-bot stepped forward. "We'll need to have a short time window. It will prevent her from being able to ask too many questions. It will keep her from getting too close to see us clearly. While we do this, you must leave this planet."

It was Jacob's turn to nod. With a rush of words, he prepared answers to the questions he thought his sister might pose, the sound of his voice echoing off the walls. He watched the bot's eyes shift with each answer they prepared.

Is it recording?

With a relieved expression, Dr. Brown inquired, "Is it agreed that the AI will impersonate you and speak with your sister while we send you and Lucy to another world? Or do you prefer being put to sleep?"

Jacob felt their gazes staring at him. "I want to say goodbye," he choked out, the words catching in his throat.

"You can't." Lucy-bot spoke, not unkindly. "This planet is about to die. You can live or die with it. There isn't time for both."

"That means you'll die, then?" The real Lucy stepped forward.

Both bots nodded. Jacob-bot spoke once more. "We knew that already. It is impossible for us to leave without throwing a new world into chaos. The remaining areas are low or no tech."

Dr. Brown asked gently, "We're out of time. Death or life?"

Lucy declared, "I choose life. Send me to wherever."

Dr. Brown called over another AI worker. "Quickly, prepare her for the final zone, please. We're running out of time."

She looked back at him. "Jacob?" her voice and eyes implored.

A sudden rush of emotion brought tears to Jacob's eyes, making his vision swim. Remembering his fight for survival and all he'd sacrificed to arrive, his mind raced. Red throwing the squirrel at him. Ella's grin around her thumb when he made faces at her. Carl, cigarette hanging from his fingers. The others lost. Bile rose as he finally accepted that he'd never see his twin again; the image of his sister's face burned into his memory. Her laughter as the dogs jumped on her, covering her with licks, when she arrived home from work. Her dramatic pretend outrage at his cheating during game nights. The smile on her face, lighting up her eyes. He had to decide.

His jaw quivered as he spoke in a gravelly voice. "Life." She would never forgive him if he chose anything else.

"Follow me, please," the AI told them.

Jacob started to follow, but stopped, looking back at the trio.

"You'll make sure she won't worry about me? That she'll be okay?"

With a synchronized nod, all three showed their agreement.

Dr. Brown responded, "Trust us. We will inform her that the decision is final and cannot be changed. We sent the remaining people while you were arguing. You are the last we can save. If you don't go now, you won't be able to. Please. Take heart in knowing she's safe. A family has taken her in. She lives."

Jacob, giving a quick nod, rejoined Lucy and followed the bot into an unfamiliar room.

Stopping in the doorway and looking back, Jacob said, "I always held being her big brother over her head, even though we're twins."

With a nod of understanding from Jacob-bot, Jacob turned and continued into the room.

"If she won't listen," Dr. Brown said, turning toward their replicas, "there is only one way to make sure she knows it's final."

Both bots nodded, turned, and went to prepare for their ultimate act for mankind. Specifically, for Jacob and Siana.

31

UPON ENTERING THE ROOM, Jacob-bot set a timer with a muted click, while Lucy-bot's fingers flew across the holographic keyboard, entering information about Setan, the country Siana had been sent to. The male bot moved to a computer, entering the number of Siana's cell phone, and sent a message with a meeting place. If the real Jacob was right, she wouldn't hesitate to go there. Since her temporal position was advanced, she would reach the field before they opened the portal. It would be the same field she woke up in.

He settled in near the designated portal location, the silence broken only by a low hum. "Start the timer when she sees me," he told his female companion. "We need to be finished before the combatant triggers the burn."

She nodded in acknowledgment while she continued to set up their plan, her fingers tapping the air of the keyboard.

"Opening now," she murmured.

Midway on the wall, a golden circle began its slow, mesmerizing rotation. The whir it made would've deafened a human within the confines of the small room. They adjusted their hearing. The portal's edges shimmered as it opened, a cool breeze emanating from within, while both bots stood still, their sensors alert, waiting. Within minutes, sunlight shone through. Both bots steeled themselves for what they must do.

A piercing "Jacob!" ripped through the air.

Jacob-bot's eyes immediately adjusted to precisely mimic Jacob's gaze as much as possible as his companion began the countdown to the fire. A fragrant breeze carried the scent of wildflowers and the earthy smell of rich soil into the shimmering portal, along with images of majestic trees. For a moment, the bot processed the data from its sensors, enjoying the novelty of this unfamiliar environment. Its creator would have been shocked to find it was beginning to feel, because it meant the bot would undergo the emotions tied to its own death.

Siana ran toward the opening, trampling flowers and grass, her footsteps muffled by the soft earth. Her clothing was the clothing she had worn when she disappeared, though she appeared much cleaner and well-fed.

He shouted, "No!" He couldn't risk her getting too close. She would notice the difference between him and her brother. "Stay!"

Her footsteps halted, her face disbelieving. "No!" she cried out and resumed running toward him.

"Stop!" he shouted, hoping she would heed his warning. She did.

"Why? I don't understand." Her face was a mask of confusion.

As the gate reached full size, just enough for a person to walk through, the noise abated.

"Jacob, what do you mean? Who is that?" Her posture shifted, and she used her hand to beckon him. "Never mind that. Come over here, please. It's safe. We can be together. We can live here. These men have been helping me." She motioned to the others.

His gaze met the shocked stares of three high-elven men, their eyes wide, and their faces pale. The closest one, a man with long dark hair and burn scars down his face, kept glancing between Siana and the opening. Six-legged steeds, their dark forms cloaked in shadow, hung back in the woods behind his "sister," snorting and pawing the ground in agitation over the shimmering portal.

"Jacob" shook his head, the weight of the world heavy on his shoulders and sadness on his face. "I will be staying here," he announced definitively. "I wanted a chance to say goodbye."

The woman turned from the console and gave Siana a sad smile.

A stunned silence replaced Sia's voice. Recovering, she inquired, "What do you mean by 'goodbye'? No, if you won't come here, then I'll come back to you." She moved toward the portal.

"I need you to listen, Sia. Please," Jacob implored.

She shook her head. "Not if it involves my not being with you. You're my only family left."

"Listen." His voice softened, a playful smile on his lips. "I'm your big brother, remember?"

A gentle breeze rustled the fragrant lavender leaves, their soft purple swaying as if waving goodbye.

"Our world is done. The AI is about to set our world on fire, killing everyone and everything. A reset."

A sharp shake of her head and a quick gesture with her hand signaled him. "Fine, then come here."

He sighed. She was making this so much harder. He understood. He really did, but her brother's strongest desire was for her to be safe. To live. Unfortunately, they were running out of time.

He shook his head, eyes begging her to understand. "I know this is hard, but you were sent here to keep you safe, but you see–I know you. I knew you wouldn't stop looking for me."

"Of course not!" Her shout rang through the field.

"Only a limited number of people can go to any one area. You and four others were sent here. Only you remain. The others didn't make it. You're the only one who has survived."

Floored, she exclaimed, "What?!"

"They don't know what happened to them. All they know is their trackers went dead. In this place, the only way that would happen is if they died. Your tracker is the only one active." He knew they could stop working for other reasons, but the world was about to end. He didn't have time to explain it all.

"Is it possible they had them removed?"

Jacob shrugged, face heavy with sadness. "We don't know. It's possible, but they just assume they're gone, not that it matters to the program." He continued, "Sending people to other places is what the friendly AI has been doing to save humans. To avoid overwhelming the population and disrupting timelines, each location has a strict quota on the number of people it can accommodate. This one had a maximum limit of five. Once it's accepted, the zone closes. No one else can go through. Even if I wanted to, I can't join you. The portal won't let me leave."

This much was true. Although they could enter at a different point in the timeline, the system would shut down specific zones after a set number of people entered during a specific time. Jacob and Lucy were the last two who could go through to the zone they were assigned. They didn't have time to set up another. If Siana came back, she would die. That went against his programming. He glanced up at the digital timer, the bright red numbers glaring down at him, counting down the seconds.

"I will go to a different area, but I need to go now. We're about out of time. It won't stay open for long. We took a risk in doing this much. I love you. Be safe. Find love. Have fat babies." His face beseeched her. "But most of all, live. I know it's cheesy, but it's what I feel."

"No, I'm coming back then!" She moved toward the portal.

Jacob-bot understood she would not give up being with her brother. He moved his hand out of Siana's view and gave a brief wave behind him at

Lucy-bot. She gave a slight nod, a silent understanding passing between them, before she surreptitiously flipped the small, almost invisible switch. They'd planned this in case she didn't accept the explanation.

A vibrant red, a blur of motion, entered the room. From Siana's perspective, the approaching machines looked like rolling execution bots—cold, hard, and lethal, each one silently heralding death. Technically, they were, but with unique programming. The holographic figures were solid to the touch, unlike typical see-through holograms, possessing a surprising weight and density. Out of the portal's limited view, the AI observed the initial trigger on the monitor. A portion of Earth ignited, a searing ring of fire spreading across its surface at an alarmingly quick rate. They had to time it perfectly.

"Jacob" turned toward the holograms, yelling at the woman to close the portal faster. With eyes widening in shock, his body crumpled to the ground as the holographic projections "shot" him. He could see Siana's dawning look of horror as she realized what she thought was happening. Her scream of denial, raw and desperate, reverberated through the still morning air of the woods. The execution bots as one turned to face her, their targeting systems seemingly locking onto her.

"Lucy's" hand slammed down on the terminal as she yelled, "No!"

At the same moment, the ring of fire reached their hideaway. An explosion, a tremendous shock wave shaking the ground and sending a blast of intense heat and pressure outwards, swallowed everything in the room. The fake Lucy and Jacob gave their last smiles as they melted and their circuitry fried, their job to humanity over. They kept their promise to the real Jacob, making sure his sister knew he was gone forever. While the AI felt regret at causing her this mental anguish, they knew it was necessary. The last sound they heard was Siana screaming Jacob's name. The raw emotion was heavy on their minds as they died and the portal closed.

32

AT THE SAME TIME, Jacob and Lucy had undergone a very rushed lesson about the world they would be landing in. It sounded exciting and scary simultaneously. For those out in the field, they'd learned the portal basically encompassed the person's tracker and the body it was contained in. It wasn't supposed to take the backpacks Phil and Siana had worn, and no one knew why it did. Dr. Brown had told them they just didn't have the time or the inclination to figure it out.

They kept the couple out of the portal room until it was ready and warned them about the sound levels. It was near where their bot doubles had gone. They received clean clothes to put on. They hurried in every movement. The AI bot had told them that those who had more time would've received lessons on the area and a full shower.

Now they looked at each other while facing the portal they would walk through. Their amazed eyes took in the opposite wall where it was located. Lucy reached out with her left hand. He took it with his right hand. Each held a duffel of clothes in the other hand, and backpacks repacked with items they may need in their new world. A hesitant smile passed between them; then, hand in hand, they walked toward it, their hearts pounding with a mixture of hope and uncertainty as they steeled themselves to begin their new lives wherever their journey took them.

They could feel the vibrations of the portal within their feet as they approached, the scene before them one of the most beautiful they'd seen in ages. Jacob's breath caught as he looked through the portal at the forest on the other side, trees of an unknown variety standing tall as if keeping guard. The room behind them began shaking with increasing intensity, a low groan echoing from within. Both paused, eyes wide with alarm, staring at each other before turning to look at the scientist.

Dr. Brown shouted, "Run! Hurry! I have to close it! We're out of time!"

They instantly obeyed, a desperate scramble for survival, the ground trembling, growing in intensity beneath their feet as their world began to crumble around them. A roar like a tornado became louder as the seconds passed. They raced to the portal, watching it slowly start to close again, seeing the brilliantly colored leaves and a field of wildflowers fading. Jacob realized it would not stay open long enough for them to reach it if they held the bags. His delay in arguing for his sister may have killed them. Jacob saw Lucy realize it too as he glanced at her.

He shouted, "Drop them! Run! Dive!"

Panicked at the thought of dying so short of their goal, they dropped their heavy duffel bags and ran, the sounds of their own harsh breathing and pounding feet filling their ears. In a blur of motion, like something out of a spy thriller, they hurled themselves through the narrow opening as the room behind them erupted in a fiery explosion, sending a wave of heat and debris in their wake.

As they ran, quickly turning, Dr. Brown hit a button and the massive program he'd prepared, written by himself and his AI comrades, activated, reseeding the planet with new life deep under the top burned layer. Once the world healed, new life would spring forth. He smiled, a quiet, self-satisfied grin, the weight of his task lifted, as his world went black.

33

LUCY'S SMILE MIRRORED JACOB'S as they watched Tenson, their son, take his first hesitant steps, the sound of his soft coos filling the air. With chubby arms outstretched, his wispy blond hair danced above his head like flames, a playful halo in the sunlight. He laughed as he lost his balance, landed on his bottom, and promptly began pulling grass. Jacob reached forward to stop him from eating it. Tenson laughed and threw it instead, causing Jacob to chuckle. So far, they had been blessed with amiable children.

The purple leaves, tinged with blue, swayed above them, the gray bark of the trees creaking with the wind. Behind them, Anna, named in part after Jacob's sister, ran, chasing a butterfly-like insect, watching it with a wisdom surpassing her five years. Her father's red curls bounced around her mother's blue eyes. Her hair was a frequent topic when people met her for the first time. This world didn't seem to have curls like hers.

After landing, and still shaken, ill and disoriented from the unexpected side effects of portal travel, exploration slowly began, each step revealing more about this alien world. The first thing they learned was that they didn't speak the same language. It took a while for them to learn to survive there. The plant life captivated Jacob. Lucy, once she realized how primitive it was, began planning on how to bring a toilet into wherever they made their home.

"I'm sick of it. I'm not going in the woods anymore that I have to," she swore to him.

While they explored, they came upon a local farmer, whose crops were being choked by unfamiliar plants. Jacob offered his assistance, even though communication was difficult, and he wasn't sure what was what. They made it work. His study of the plants helped him understand which were planted and which grew wild. Jacob posited that birds probably dropped seeds of the weed from another area, and it took root here. It took him almost two weeks, during which the farmer let them sleep in his barn and fed them once a day, but he eventually figured out a solution that would remove the plants yet keep the fields intact. Part of that involved identifying the young plant before its roots became entangled with the farmer's crop.

His successful help earned them enough grateful payment to buy durable clothes that fit in better with the local culture and much-needed supplies. The farmer had taken them into town, helping them navigate the haggling, since merchants liked to take advantage of foreigners. They moved on to another town, though both were heartily sick of walking everywhere, and then another.

In a larger town, someone overheard one of the town's rulers expressing interest in bringing water to the healing centers. Lucy had volunteered her services, which caused a few raised eyebrows. It didn't take long for them to realize that not only did she not put up with that nonsense, she knew what she was talking about. She designed a simple hose system that utilized both rain catchment and the local lake. She showed them how to filter the water, boil it, and put it in a sealed barrel for later use.

Her help caused Jacob and her to receive quite a large reward. That payment had supported them for a while. It didn't take long for the couple to realize that their expertise in a low-tech area was in high demand. Jobs had steamrolled between the two as they traveled the area, and eventually a town that didn't want to lose their knowledge awarded them an enormous plot of land to the north of the town proper, near the base of a small mountain range.

Jacob and Lucy had given back by hiring the local mason to build a small starter home of stone and wood while they decided how they wanted to lay out their new estate. Jacob, of course, wouldn't start any building until he had learned the flora. He wanted to make sure they left potential food sources. The skills they had learned on the run came in handy from the moment they landed.

They took on other jobs over time, some involving travel, and eventually hired numerous artisans to complete construction on their newly finished estate. Jacob had insisted it had to be built behind a river and have a drawbridge for attacks and secret passages. Lucy had simply rolled her eyes and let him have his way. Now they lived in comfort. They'd achieved a status they never would have on

Earth. Jacob had begun to get involved in local politics.

Their fundamental problem had been the language. They had a difficult start, but through persistent effort, they achieved near-native fluency. They raised their children bilingually, filling their home with the sounds of both languages. All three slipped between each seamlessly, though Anna liked to mix hers up, confusing many a guest.

"Sir, I'm sorry to interrupt."

Jacob, turning to his servant, asked, "What is it?"

"A letter, sir. I was told to give it to you immediately."

Jacob took the letter from the outstretched hand. "Thank you."

He opened it and skimmed the contents as the man left.

With a playful arch of one eyebrow, the sound of their son's sweet, unintelligible chatter at whatever serious topic occupied his mind caused Lucy to grin.

"It's a letter from the Clan leader thanking us for our help. Though to be fair, it was all you." Jacob smiled wryly.

As she took and cradled the letter, she read it. Lucy stated, "Well, you identified the plants causing the blockage."

He shrugged. "Teamwork makes the dream work."

Her response was to roll her eyes at him. They sat, each lost in their thoughts as the children played. Lucy leaned against her husband.

"What are you thinking?" she asked, tilting her head back to look at him.

"How a simple camping trip turned into all this," he answered quietly, his arm sweeping the surrounding area. They both listened to the quiet punctuated by bird and insect song and the sound of their children's voices. The sun dipped below the treetops and prompted Lucy to gather their protesting son into her arms.

Jacob called, "Come, Anna. It's time to go home."

He watched as she ran back. The red and yellow dress swirled around her legs as she turned toward her parents. Jacob, swinging her into his arms, couldn't help but wonder how her namesake was. He hoped she was happy, wherever she was, as much as he had become.

Sandy West

Thank you!

Thank you for reading! If you enjoyed the book and would like to support the author, please leave feedback on Goodreads, Amazon, or both. It helps boosts an author's book.

If you'd like to follow me on social media, you can join me on:

Facebook: @authorsandywest
X: @authorsandywest

I'm curious to know how many connections readers caught between each book.

Sandy West

About the author:

Sandy lives on a farmstead in Texas. When she's not writing, she crochets, reads, and plays video games with her adult children in addition to taking care of her dogs, horses, donkeys, chickens, sheep, goats and turkeys. She can be reached via her contacts on her listed social media.

Facebook: @authorsandywest

X: @authorsandywest

Sandy West